I0612400

CROSSING

the

DEAD HEART

C.T. MADIGAN

ETT IMPRINT

Exile Bay

This 5th edition published by ETT IMPRINT, Exile Bay 2023

First published in Australia in 1946 by Georgian House.
Reprinted 1948.
Revised edition published by Rigby Limited in 1974.
New edition published by JB Books in 2001.

Copyright © ETT Imprint 2023

This book is copyright.

Apart from any fair dealing for the purposes of private study, research, criticism or review, as permitted under the Copyright Act, no part may be reproduced by any process without written permission. Inquiries should be addressed to the publishers.

ISBN 978-1-923024-06-9 (pbk)
ISBN 978-1-923024-07-6 (ebk)

Cover: *The Andado Mail*. An engineless camel-drawn motor car which never breaks down. Fred Sharpe at the wheel.

Cover and internal design by Tom Thompson

CONTENTS

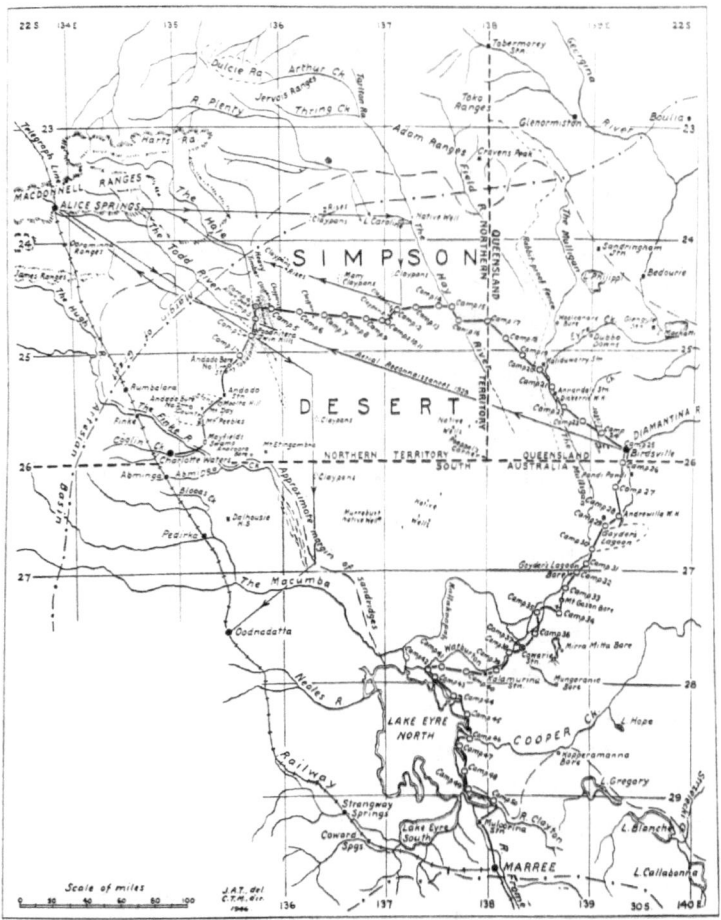

Route of the expedition

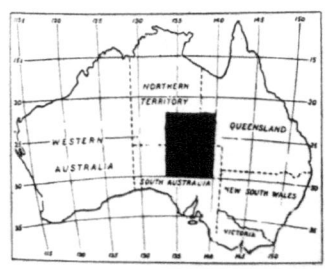

PREFACE

THIS book is a popular narrative of the Simpson Desert Expedition, 1939. The scientific results are being published by the Royal Society of South Australia, and papers have already appeared on the physiography and meteorology, the mineralogy of the desert sands, the sand formations, the spiders, the fishes, the reptiles, some of the insects, part of the botany (the catalogue of plants), and the soils and vegetation. These will be found in volumes 68, 69, and 70 of the *Transactions* of the Society. Among papers still to come are the description of the main insect collection, a comparative study of the desert flora, and notes on the mammals and birds.

The scientific papers are mainly technical descriptions, of interest chiefly to specialists in the various subjects; this narrative gives the general story of the Expedition, with no more scientific detail than is of general interest. It is a plain tale of what was actually seen and done, without dramatization or exaggeration. There were no high adventures, which are usually due to incompetence or invention, but the spirit of adventure was not lacking. There was enough risk to give colour to the enterprise, and enough strange variety to keep the glamour of the desert undimmed from day to day. Those things, if they can be adequately conveyed, together with the human interest, make the story of the Expedition a tale worth telling.

The Expedition owed its existence to the late Mr. A. A. Simpson, C.M.G., of Adelaide, after whom the desert was originally named. The enterprise was carried out at his suggestion and was entirely financed by him. Grateful acknowledgment is also made to the following for their contributions to the success of the Expedition:

To the University of Adelaide, for granting the necessary leave of absence.

To the Australian Broadcasting Commission and The Advertiser Newspapers Limited, who gave helpful co-operation and publicity to the Expedition.

To Bejah Dervish and his son Jack Bejah and the Afghans of Marree, who exercised such care in the selection and provision of an excellent camel team and equipment.

To Mr. A. H. Traeger, O.B.E., who provided us with one of his pedal wireless sets, which proved a complete success.

To Mr. H. E. Ding, of Yunta, who handled all the wireless traffic through his station V.H.U9. This included transcribing many press and private messages for telegraphing, and the organization of the reception and relaying of the national broadcasts, which latter would have been impossible without him. In addition he gave much useful advice on the operation of our own set.

To Messrs. W. Angliss & Co. (Aust.) Pty. Ltd., who supplied several cases of "Imperial" tinned meats, which were accepted as a luxury but proved to be a necessity.

To the Royal Society of South Australia, for publishing the scientific reports.

And finally, to all my comrades of the journey, who went laughing through a wilderness.

C. T. MADIGAN.
Blackwood, August 1946.

1

THE SIMPSON DESERT, LAST UNTRODDEN AREA IN AUSTRALIA

AS long ago as 1927 my geological explorations and investigations in Central Australia were begun. Everything that had been published by explorers or geologists on the central regions was soon read, and these researches coupled with enquiries among the pastoralists, drovers, miners and adventurers I had met in the Centre, convinced me that there was still one patch of Australia where the white man's foot had never trodden, and that was the sandridge desert in the south-eastern corner of the Northern Territory, north of Lake Eyre. The sandridges made the use of motor transport, at least the kind of motor transport available in this country, impossible, while the lack of feed and water had prevented penetration by pack horse or even camels. This desert is only some three hundred miles across, which is not an impossible dry stage for camels if some green feed is available for them, yet it appeared that the endless succession of sandridges had presented such difficulties and proved so exhausting that even attempts to cross by camel had been abandoned.

All my enquiries in every direction failed to discover any evidence that these attempts had ever resulted in anything but a mere nibbling at the margins. Jim O'Neill, the famous opal prospector, had tried to go eastward from, the Hay River and had turned back in a sea of sandridges and spinifex. Simon Rieff, miner and prospector of Alice Springs, had gone across the top end to Lake Caroline on the Hay River, in a dry season, and had lost most of his camels and barely escaped with his life. Everywhere the tale was the same on the western side of the desert, where my first enquiries were made.

Here then was an interesting bit of exploration to be done, to find out what lay lay behind the forbidding borders of this unknown area, and the aeroplane was the obvious means of solving the problem.

In 1929 I obtained the support of the Royal Geographical Society of Australasia, South Australian Branch, for a project to carry out an aerial reconnaissance of the dry lakes of South Australia and the unknown desert regions to the north of them, and also to make aerial geological investigations in the Mac Donnell Ranges. The publicity this expedition received in the press brought forth a crop of letters in the papers from bushmen and some others who should have been better informed, deriding my "unknown area". One man claimed that he had taken racehorses to Alice Springs from Queensland across this "desert"; another that he had been marooned up gum trees by the floods in the "desert". The old bushman is inclined to be resentful of the "amateur explorer" or new-comer in his special field, and he is always jealous of his own knowledge of the country. His great disadvantage is that he is not familiar with maps. Most of the writers showed that they were talking of some other part of the inland regions and not the area under discussion, actually providing evidence that the desert really was unknown.

I was not on as firm ground then, for my work had only begun, and I was a little shaken by some of the claims put forward by men still living in the country, but after later travels, when I had made enquiries on the cattle stations all round the desert, and even learned something of the critics themselves, I was completely satisfied that at that time no man had crossed this desert, and all that was known of it was what could be conjectured by visiting its margins.

Even my old friend, the late Larry Wells, the explorer, had his hit at me by writing that the few hundred miles across this desert would be nothing to camels. He had surveyed the Queensland-Northern Territory border, the eastern side of the desert, and also made his great journey from Willuna to the Fitzroy River across the Great Sandy Desert in Western Australia, and he knew camels and sandhills. He wrote another letter to *The Advertiser* saying that he did not mean to "wound" Dr. Madigan, but he proceeded to elaborate his point, and with his knowledge and experience he did my credit in men's eyes some harm. Larry knew only the eastern side of the desert, where the sandridges are scarcely an obstacle at all; no one knew the interior. It was a great regret to me that he did not live to hear the story I am now going to tell.

However, this was away back in 1929, and I was in truth a beginner, though more right than I knew then.

The aerial reconnaissance was arranged with the help of the Geographical Society and the co-operation of the Royal Australian Air Force, who put two of their then newly-arrived Wapiti aeroplanes with crews at my disposal. This was the first time that the Eagle cameras had been used in this country, and we took the first aerial strip photographs. It was also the first time that aeroplanes had been used for geological work in the Commonwealth. The results of this expedition were published in the *Proceedings of the Royal Geographical Society of Australasia, South Australian Branch, Vol. 30, 1928-29.*

During the expedition three flights were made over the unknown area; the first direct from Birdsville to Alice Springs, the second eastward from Alice Springs to Lake Caroline, thence fifty miles southward and direct back to Alice Springs, and the third south-eastward from Alice Springs to the centre of the desert and then south to Oodnadatta. Many vertical and oblique photographs were taken, but there had been little to photograph. Some claypanswere seen in the northern parts of the desert and some water-courses, not hitherto mapped, near the margins, but all the rest was a uniform monotony of sandridges and spinifex. There were no ranges hidden behind the sandridge ramparts, no water, nothing to record from the air but some slight changes in the relative sparseness of the vegetation. The whole expanse below was like a pink and gigantic circular gridiron, ribbed with close straight sandridges from horizon to horizon. The sandridges were remarkably uniformly spaced, being about a quarter of a mile apart, and their narrowness, straightness and continuity were unique and astonishing. Their trend was about 30o west of north, and they ran straight as far as the eye could see, which was some fifty miles in each direction from 4,000 feet. Their uniformity and parallelism were much more obvious and arresting as seen on the smaller scale from the air than appeared later from the ground, where local irregularities tend to obscure the general plan and the view is limited to a single lane between two sandridges if you are in a lane, or to two lanes if you are on a crest.

At the close of this expedition I said that there seemed to be nothing to warrant the expenditure of any further effort in the exploration of this desert as it contained nothing but sandridges, and all that was to be found there, could be seen round its borders. The late Mr. A. A. Simpson, C.M.G., of Adelaide, was the president of the Geographical Society at that time and had been most helpful in the preliminary arrangements. He said he would not object to having his name attached to so inhospitable a region, so I named the Simpson Desert after him, and the name was duly accepted by the Department of the Interior, Canberra.

The Simpson Desert is a unique physiographical unit whose borders are clearly defined. It is a vast level plain of some 56,000 square miles, a waste ribbed with parallel sandridges and sparsely clothed with spinifex, the commonest and universal plant. It lies roughly between latitude 23° and 27o south and longitude 135° and 139° east. It is waterless except in times of rain, when streams enter it from the northwest, but all these streams soon flood out in it, with none reaching the farther side. It forms a broad triangle with the apex on Lake Eyre in the south. Its margins are the Finke and Macumba Rivers on the west, the Mac Donnell Ranges to the north-west, the Plenty and Thring (Marshall) Rivers to the north, the Mulligan River to the east, and the lower Diamantina and Kallakoopah Rivers in the south.

It lies mostly in the south-east corner of the Northern Territory, but extends into Queensland and South Australia. Sand and spinifex are its dominant characteristics, and here let us deal with this matter of spinifex once and for all, so that it will not be necessary to be continually and pedantically referring to the so-called spinifex, like the people who talk about the so-called crow. The genus spinifex is mainly a coastal sand-dune grass, civilized and tractable. It is represented in the desert by a species known as cane grass, *Spinifex paradoxus*. The universal spiky, hemispherical masses typical of the whole of the Central Australian sandy deserts belong to another genus, *Triodia*, a much more forbidding plant, among which even camels and horses pick their way. The commonest species is *Triodia basedowi*. Its popular name is more properly porcupine grass, but spinifex has become attached to it and we will let it stay. It is too late to tell David Carnegie that his book should have been called "Porcupine and Sand".

On this aerial expedition many new contacts were made with pastoralists on the eastern side of the desert, notably Mr. L. Reese of Birdsville, who had a lifetime's experience of the Queensland border regions. He was certain that no white man had crossed the desert, and was convinced from frequent questioning that the blacks did not go far in either, but had a wholesome fear of the area.

In the same year I followed up the aerial investigations of Lake Eyre by a ground expedition to the lake, which was at that time completely dry. This gave an opportunity of gathering more information on the Lake Eyre Basin and its stock routes.

In 1935 and 1937 I traversed the northern end of the desert, through the Jervois, Tarlton and Toko Ranges. A dogger, Fred Rogers, who had lived for ten years in that most isolated spot where the Thring and Arthur Creeks join to form the Hay River, gave very interesting and useful information on the nature of the unmapped country to the south of him. He and his natives would go down the Hay in wet seasons but would not leave its vicinity. From his camp we made a day's excursion into the desert on horses.

By this time I had travelled almost all round the desert, had flown over most of it, and got to know the inhabitants round its borders. It was obvious that the drovers who thought they had crossed it had merely gone round it either on the north side from Tobermorey Station in Queensland via the Jervois Ranges to Alice Springs, where there are no sandridges, or on the south side from Birdsville down the Diamantma and up the Macumba, the latter not a difficult stock route.

In response to an invitation from the Royal Society of New South Wales to give the Clarke Memorial Lecture for 1938, I chose as my subject "The Simpson Desert and its Borders," and this lecture, later published in the journal of the society for that year, gave all my knowledge of the desert up to that time.

At the close of this lecture my earlier statements that there was nothing to warrant further investigation of the Simpson Desert were modified. Its broader features were certainly known, but it still had not been crossed on the ground. Comparison was made with the much bigger problem of Mt. Everest, whose summit had been seen and photographed from the air and whose base had been studied from the ground, surely leaving nothing more to be discovered about it, yet man must set his foot on the topmost point. All is not known about new environments till man has had the personal experience of living in them, and there is great satisfaction in overcoming the natural obstacles and discovering the adjustments necessary to make this possible. The Simpson Desert should be crossed on foot, from west to east across its centre. This would give the fullest details of the arrangement and nature of the remarkable series of parallel sandridges whose origin and mode of formation were still a puzzle, as well as provide an opportunity for a complete study of the fauna and flora of a unique desert area. Geographically the field was restricted, but in the natural sciences such a journey still presented great attraction and possibilities.

The distance across the difficult central part of the desert was only about three hundred miles, and the requirements were good camels and a good season when it could reasonably be expected that green herbage would be found, for then the camels could do the journey without water, which it was anticipated they would have to do. Given a good season, the only remaining hazard was the ability of the camels to stand up to the heavy work of continually struggling across the sandridges, which had steep banks of loose sand along their crests.

Ever since the aerial investigations, Mr. Simpson had been anxious that his desert should be further explored on the ground, but I had been unwilling, as I felt that to make it worthwhile a well organized and equipped expedition including botanists and biologists was necessary, something considerably more elaborate and costly than my two-man journeys of the past had been. The use of helicopters had been suggested but was rejected as being too hazardous and impracticable at that stage of development of the helicopter. Short demonstration flights with one of these machines were being given in Australia at the time. The most primitive and ancient means of transport in the desert—the camel —was undoubtedly the safest, the surest, the most effective, and not least, the cheapest, for this task.

After the Clarke Memorial Lecture, Mr. Simpson approached me again, and I drew up a plan for a camel expedition across the desert at an estimated cost of £500 to cover equipment, stores, camel and truck hire, rail travel and incidentals, the scientific staff to receive only their out-of-pocket expenses, and as much as possible of the instruments and scientific equipment to be borrowed. Mr. Simpson agreed to finance this expedition.

The 1937-38 season in the interior had been a phenomenally wet one, with floods and washaways along the railway line. Herbage was abundant. Another good season to follow could be anticipated from past experiences of the vagaries of the weather, as there are usually two good seasons in succession, so that the time seemed most propitious, and preparations were begun in the middle of 1938 for an expedition to start out in the winter of 1939. Crossing the sandridges in the summer, when the desert is no place for any kind of human activities, would be impossible, even for camels. The difference between summer and winter in these regions has to be experienced to be believed. The heat makes the summer almost unbearable, but in winter the weather is perfect by day, clear, sunny and bracing, while the nights are so cold that it is a common mistake not to take enough blankets to make sleep possible.

The Andado Mail. An engineless camel-drawn motor car which never breaks down. Fred Sharpe at the wheel.

2

EARLIER ATTEMPTS TO CROSS THE DESERT

AS a background for our journey, it will be of interest to review the earlier explorations in the area and the previous attempts to cross the desert. The desert was first seen and entered by Sturt in 1845 in his attempt to reach the centre of the continent from a point on the Darling River where Menindie now stands. He discovered and named the Barrier Ranges, the Strzelecki, Cooper and Eyre Creeks, and was finally defeated when within two hundred miles of his goal by the waterless sea of sandridges and spinifex in which he found himself, the Simpson Desert. He turned back at a point near the present Queensland border in latitude 24° 40' S., on the more hospitable eastern side of the desert.

To modify modern slang, he had not seen anything yet, though he wrote: "It was a remarkable fact that here on the northern side of the desert (his Stony Desert, in the Diamantina country) and after an interval of more than fifty miles, the same sandridges should occur, running in parallel lines at the same angle as before into the very heart of the interior, as if they absolutely were never to terminate", and at his turning point, "We had penetrated to a point at which water and feed had both failed. Spinifex and a new species of Mesembryanthemum .... were the only plants growing in that wilderness, if I except a few withered acacia trees about four feet high. The spinifex was close and matted, and the horses were obliged to lift their feet straight up to avoid its sharp points. From the summit of a sandy undulation close upon our right we saw that the ridges extended northwards in parallel lines beyond the range of vision, and appeared as if interminable. To the eastward and westward they succeeded each other like the waves of the sea. The sand was of a deep red colour, and a bright narrow line of it marked the top of each ridge, amidst the sickly pink and glaucous-coloured vegetation around". These few vivid words, written nearly a hundred years ago, proved to be an accurate description of the whole of the 56,000 square miles of the Simpson Desert, yet an account of the journeys that have led up to this conclusion make a tale worth telling. It would have been fatal for Sturt to have attempted to continue on his course with his horses, and difficult enough with camels, though he was running parallel to the sandridges and not across them.

Next Burke and Wills made their ill-managed and fatal expedition up the eastern side of the desert. They were the first to visit the lower Cooper, but their records were too meagre to be of any value. It was the relief expeditions sent out after them that really advanced the knowledge of the country, and particularly the one from Adelaide led by J. McKinley in 1861-2. He went right through to the Gulf of Carpentaria, and his reports led to the occupation of the Cooper and Diamantina country in South Australia.

In 1876 the Queensland Government sent out an expedition under W. O. Hodgkinson, who had been in McKinlay's party, to explore the western side of the State. He discovered the Mulligan River and the Toko Range, which he originally named the Cairns Range. This journey completed the preliminary exploration of the eastern side of the Simpson Desert.

J. W. Lewis in 1874-75 first sketch-mapped most of the shores of Lake Eyre, a task still incomplete, and carried his route surveys up the Warburton and Diamantina to beyond where Birdsville now stands, thus delineating the south-eastern margin of the desert. Other South Australian surveyors, H. Vere Barclay and C. Winnecke in the years 1878-81 rounded the northern end of the desert and discovered the Plenty, Marshall, Thring and Arthur rivers and the Jervois and Tarlton Ranges. The western margin of the mapped country was still the Overland Telegraph route, first traversed by MacDouall Stuart in 1861. The telegraph line was completed in 1872.

In 1883 Winnecke, with camels, made the first definite attempt to examine the desert itself. He came in from Queensland and traversed most of the upper course of the Hay River, which he discovered and named after a Queensland pastoralist. He made considerable diversions on each side of the river. His traverses remained the eastern limits of ground exploration of the Simpson Desert and there is no evidence that the lower Hay had ever been visited by anyone except Winnecke till we arrived there in 1939. Winnecke wrote that: "This country is a perfect desert and I am afraid will never be of much use to the squatter. I am almost certain that this country has never been visited by natives".

At one stage his camels travelled 278 miles in sixteen days without water in what Winnecke described as the heaviest and worst sandhill country in Australia.

The Queensland-Northern Territory border was surveyed between 1883 and 1886. L. A. Wells was assistant surveyor throughout and never left the task from beginning to end. He said he was granted a fortnight's leave at the end of it, but this was cancelled and he was sent out on another urgent survey job immediately on his return to Adelaide. Hard old days indeed, but they made men. Wells used to check the chaining by taking latitudes with a sextant by meridian altitudes of stars, staying up all night to take twenty north and twenty south stars. This would seem to be checking accurate methods by approximate ones, but no doubt the relative values change places when it is a matter of dragging the hundred jingling links of the old Gunter's chain over seven hundred miles of sandhill and scrub. He said that they put in a low but solid peg every quarter of a mile and a good post at every mile, with the mileage from Poeppel's Corner marked on it. The boundary between the Northern Territory and South Australia, westward from Poeppel's Corner (Poeppel was the surveyor who started the north-south line) along the 26th parallel across the Simpson Desert, has never been surveyed.

David Lindsay in 1885 set out on an unsuccessful attempt to cross the desert from south to north. He first managed to get across the southern end of the desert from Dalhousie Springs, using a native guide who knew a line of waterholes or native wells stringing across and ending among the claypans near Poeppel's Corner. He then tried to go north-eastward from the bend in the Finke where Anacoora Bore now is, but gave up the attempt after three days, considering that the task was too much for the camels, owing to the sandridges and the intense heat.

In 1916 the late Surveyor-General of South Australia, T. E. Day, made the journey from Charlotte Waters to the point where the Todd and Hale Rivers flood out, and then one party followed the Hale up into the Mac Donnell Ranges. Day's journey up the Hale set the western margin of authentically described country, Winnecke's journeys along the Thring

(Marshall) and Hay the northern and eastern margins and Lindsay's tracks the south-western and southern margins when I made my aerial reconnaissances in 1929.

Since then, in 1936, Mr. E. A. Colson, a pastoralist of Blood's Creek, made a very successful southern crossing of the desert with one black boy and camels, travelling from Mt, Etingambra near Anacoora Bore to Poeppel's Corner and Birdsville, and returning on a more southerly route. His journeys lay immediately north of Lindsay's track, and he was the first to traverse the vicinity of the 26th parallel, the border line between the Territory and South Australia. Mr. Colson later planned to cross the middle of the desert from the end of the Hale River, the route I had selected for 1939. He actually started out, but had to abandon the project before reaching the Hale through lack of equipment and apparently the consequent dissatisfaction of the party, who were all very inexperienced. The routes of all these journeys, including my flights, are shown on the map accompanying the Clarke Memorial Lecture referred to above.

Anacoora Bore was sunk many years ago with a view to opening a stock route across the desert from Queensland. My old friend Charlie Kunoth was employed on it. He told me that he went eastward from the bore seventy miles with Surveyor Ayliffe and camels to select another bore site. They found the country so inhospitable that no further bores were sunk and the stock route project was abandoned.

An adventurer named Bryce Russell boasted that he could cross the Simpson Desert alone, and started out from Oodnadatta with camels in the winter of 1937, in defiance of all warnings. Officially he has never been heard of since. Extensive searches for him were carried out by the Royal Australian Air Force. He wrote to me on the day of his departure from Oodnadatta saying that it would be hopeless to look for him if he did not turn up. It seemed very much as if the whole thing was staged as a means of effecting a disappearance as complete as that of Leichhardt, particularly as it was rumoured that he turned up soon after in Queensland.

This, then, is the story of the Simpson Desert up to the time of the Simpson Desert Expedition of 1939.

3

PREPARATIONS

THE success of an expedition depends primarily on the preliminary organization. Stefansson has rightly said that adventures are a sign of incompetence. In these days, when no terrestrial conditions are quite unknown, success should be assured before an expedition sets out 5 nothing unexpected should happen, no difficulties should arise that the party is not prepared to meet and defeat. Many explorers have said that their greatest difficulties and worries were endured before ever they set sail, and once all equipment and party were on board the rest was comparatively easy. This is a profound truth, but the preliminaries are not all worry and trouble 5 finance is usually the worst obstacle; the planning, the basis of the whole enterprise, is of absorbing interest, and the satisfaction later of seeing the plans work out successfully in the field is unsurpassed. It is a pleasure missed by those who only take part in the carrying-out, for to them it is all just plain sailing.

This expedition was a small one; the objective was of no great importance, the times and distances were unimpressive; yet it set out to do something that had not been done before, a task that had been attempted half a dozen times by men of experience over a period of a hundred years. Former attempts had all ended in failure and in some cases possibly in loss of life. This little desert was obviously a tough nut to crack, and the journey was not one to be lightly undertaken.

The route was to be from Charlotte Waters up northward through Andado Station to the junction of the Hale and Todd Rivers and thence eastward across the middle of the desert to the Mulligan River in Queensland, and thence to Birdsville. Andado Bore would probably be the last water before reaching the on the other side of the desert, so that a waterless stage of some two hundred and fifty miles had to be reckoned on. Camels, whose natural environment is the desert, were the surest means of transport, and the first thing to do was to find a good camel team. Thoughts at once turned to

Bejah Dervish, Larry Wells' old camel man on all his desert journeys, who was still living at Marree. There were camels at Marree, where the Afghans were still able to find some employment for them, so I visited Bejah in August of 1938. I found him the grand old man Larry Wells had always represented him to be, still full of tales of the great adventure of the journey of the Calvert Expedition of 1896-7 from Willuna to the Fitzroy across the Great Sandy Desert in Western Australia, and proud to tell that Wells had called him his friend. Bejah said with great regret that he was too old to go, but his son Jack, who was away at the time, would go, and Jack was a good boy on whom I could rely. He had a big round-up of camels to show me and there were obviously plenty to choose from. The only uncertain quantity was Jack, whom I did not see till the following February, when I made another trip to Marree for that purpose. Jack Bejah impressed me favourably at once. He was young, solidly built and powerful, and seemed keen on the undertaking. He had his own camel team which he used on stations and fencing jobs in the outback, and could make up the required number from his friends' herds in Marree, where there seemed to be a sort of pool of camels, mostly out of work. Jack was tough, knew camels and the country, and seemed just the man for the job. Indeed, he later thoroughly proved himself to be a worthy son of his father. He was one of the first members appointed to the party, and he could not have been a better choice.

After the camels came the party, and this presented difficulties, as there were to be no salaries, and few men of the required qualifications could leave their work for three months. The smallest party should contain at least a botanist, a biologist, a photographer, and a wireless operator, with myself as leader, navigator and geologist, and possibly a cook.

To my great satisfaction my old friend and former student, R. L, Crocker, was able to get leave from his duties as a soil surveyor for the Council for Scientific and Industrial Research at the Waite Institute to come with me as botanist. We had been round the northern end of the desert together before and he already had some experience of the desert flora. R. A. Simpson, the son of the expedition's patron, was anxious to come, and he fitted in excellently as wireless operator. The field biologist was more difficult. Eventually H. O. Fletcher, palaeontologist at the Australian Museum, Sydney, was appointed. He had been an assistant biologist on one of Mawson's summer cruises in the Antarctic, and had had some experience as assistant collector for the Museum in the Northern Territory. A man experienced with the moving picture camera was required, but no professional photographer could be persuaded to come. Photography is a very important part of any expedition, and it requires to have one man with his mind continually on it, and with an eye to what makes a picture, or opportunities are lost never to return. A primary maxim is, never miss a picture in the hope that the chance will recur under better conditions. Experience in making a photographic record of ever-changing scenes is much more important than is generally known; it is not sufficient to be able to handle a camera. A young friend of Simpson's, David Marshall, was finally appointed.

If the scientists are to have full opportunity to do their work, a cook is necessary. On my small journeys in the interior I had always done my own cooking, but decided this time to take a cook, and it was a happy decision, for Albert Hubbard, who had heard of the proposed expedition, came and offered his services free of charge, and he proved to be one of the outstanding successes of the expedition. He had been cook both at hotels and shearing sheds and knew what was required and how to do it. When every day is a day of travel most of the scientific work has to be done at camping time and it is a great help to the scientists to be relieved by a cook of the task of preparing meals during the last hour or two of daylight, not to mention the improvement in the meals, which otherwise are apt to be left till they have to be prepared in the dark by tired men. Napoleon's famous saying applies not only to armies.

Once the camels and the party were assured, the next thing to consider was equipment. Bejah had shown me a shed full of the best camel pack saddles I had ever seen, all strong and in excellent repair. The Arab pack saddle is always a lamentable affair, just on the point of falling to pieces, and held together with odd bits of much-frayed cordage which parts at the least pull. All Arab repairs are temporary, till in time the whole saddle becomes temporary, with the straw protruding from much-patched sacking and the bars continually falling off. Bejah's saddle pads were very heavily stuffed and covered on the underside with genuine imported Indian goat-hair the ideal material, and not a straw was to be seen. The wooden frames were strong and very well made. It needed only a glance at the saddles to reassure me that I was not going to have anything to worry about in the matter of baggage transport. There was, however, a shortage of riding saddles, and here I was able to rely on my friends the police at Alice Springs, whose equipment I had often used before and knew to be very good, having been designed for personal use rather than for baggage camel trains. The police had iron-framed riding saddles and great leather saddle-bags for them, and also very strong iron-bound wooden tucker boxes for baggage camels that could be used for instruments and other scientific gear such as collecting bottles. I have never seen better equipment for its purpose than the gear of the Northern Territory Police Camel Patrols. It had often been admired by other camel men in my former journeys; now it was falling into disuse as the motor car replaced the camel, so the Administrator gave me all I wanted, four riding saddles with saddle bags, to which I had only to add some new girths and stirrup irons and leathers, and four camel boxes. With this patrol gear and Bejah's pack saddles I had most excellent camel equipment, and so efficient was it that even after crossing a thousand sandridges and making more than fifty camps, not a thing was damaged, though our load included a ship's chronometer, theodolite, compasses, cameras, batteries, many bottles, wireless valves, and lamp globes. Much gear was borrowed and all was insured, yet we could not find an excuse to make a single claim on the insurance company when the expedition ended!

Water was expected to be our chief problem, and provision to meet it was a fundamental part of the planning. I reckoned that we might be out of reach of any water supply for perhaps three weeks, and for this period we must carry all the water we needed. The party would consist of nine men, and a gallon a day should be ensured, so that we must load up with about two hundred gallons of water; for this, fourteen sixteen-gallon galvanized iron camel canteens were made to my own design. They were very successful, and were in great demand at the close of the expedition. In addition, there were a pair of 4-gallon canteens for emergency use on short journeys in case it was necessary to send a detachment away from the main party. A coil of copper tubing was also taken to make a condenser in case we got into difficulties and should find water in salt lakes. A condenser could readily have been rigged up by luting the end of the coil into the bung of a canteen with clay, but it would be very difficult without a metal tube. Happily the coil was never required.

A pair of 16-gallon canteens would make about a four-hundred pound load for a camel, which was a reasonable maximum for sandridge travelling, though half a ton is not an uncommon load for Australian camels, and even up to four 360-lb. bales of wool is sometimes carried. Seven camels were thus needed for water, seven for riding and carrying the rider's personal gear, and five should take the rest of the stores and equipment, so that we required nineteen good camels.

The low cost of the expedition was due in part to the generous assistance of various bodies in the loan of equipment, or in some cases the promise of re-purchase on return. The wireless equipment was one of Traeger's pedal sets, made in Adelaide. These excellent little outfits were in use at many homesteads throughout the Interior; in fact there was a regular network of internal communication in the north-east of South Australia and through Birdsville into Queensland. Harry Ding of Yunta on the Broken Hill railway line seemed to exercise a sort of local control in his area, and Bob Gaffney filled a similar role at Birdsville. Ding was running an inland motor transport service and had all his trucks equipped with these Traeger sets so that he could keep in touch with them, and they report any trouble to him. He had the whole set-up of wireless communication at his finger ends, including much experience in care and maintenance, which proved very valuable to us, and it was soon arranged that our channel of communication with the outside world should be through him and his more elaborate receiving station at Yunta on the telegraph line. He arranged to receive and transmit all our messages, including national broadcasts from the desert, and our wireless success was very largely due to him and his organization. The Traeger set is very light and consists of the pedal generator and necessary valve equipment, and a small aerial with telescopic poles. We also carried batteries which were found quite adequate and lasted the journey through, so that the pedal generator was scarcely used. The range was up to a thousand miles at night. Yunta was six hundred miles from us and we never failed to make contact at night.

As well as prismatic compasses I took a Sestrel Mark 111A aerial compass of the kind commonly used on commercial planes, which I attached permanently to my camel saddle on a board in front of me and half-way between the iron frames of the saddle, the slight effect of which was readily compensated, This was an excellent arrangement in theory, as the compass is very easy to read and courses can be readily set, as with a ship's compass, but in practice the motion of the camel makes this type of liquid compass rather too sluggish and it was not an unqualified success. When swung out of true it tended to stay there and one was never quite sure at a glance whether it was going to move again or not. A good deal of checking had to be done by stopping and using the prismatic.

The University of Adelaide lent a theodolite, an Abney level, and two petrol lamps. The South Australian Government and the Board of Anthropological Research each provided a 16 mm. moving picture camera. Among the purchases were the ship's chronometer, an aneroid barometer, tapes, maximum and minimum thermometers, firearms and other small instruments. Several members of the party brought their own hand cameras. The Australian Museum provided the collecting bottles and spirit cans and other biological equipment.

We had no medical man, but I took my usual little kit of things that experience has shown meet the bushman's needs, things that are fool-proof but may be a very present help. It consisted of bandages, gauze and medicated dressings, eye- bath, scissors, tweezers, boracic acid, iodine, Condy's crystals, aspirin, antiseptic ointment, laxative pills, chlorodyne and snake-bite outfit.

The value of the snake-bite outfit, a little wooden tube with a scarifier at one end and some Condy's crystals to rub in at the other, probably does not extend beyond, the psychological effect of having it with you, a value not to be altogether despised. Chlorodyne is a very popular outback remedy, stocked by every store. It is a pain killer, used to alleviate "belly-ache". Sometimes it is taken excessively as a narcotic. The only things that we actually used on the expedition were a bandage and some ointment on a blistered heel, and someone took a few drops of chlorodyne, probably to see what it was like.

The camp equipment was simple. All that the drover uses in rain or shine is his blankets and 10 feet by 10 feet Birkmyre waterproof canvas sheet. The sheet encloses all his belongings and makes the "swag". Besides the sheets, canvas sleeping bags were also provided for those of the party who did not already have them, but they were not necessary. The sheet is all that could be desired. It can be laid on brushwood if the ground is wet. To make the bed the sheet is first spread on the ground and the blankets laid out on one half. The other half is then lapped over the bed, and may be tucked under all round if there is rain; and there is nothing in the same class as the Birkmyre canvas; the bushman will not look at anything else. I had not used these sheets before, and thought that 10 feet by 8 feet looked quite sufficient, but I was wrong; the two extra feet are needed, and 10 by 10 is the perfect size. We took no stretchers or tents, but included an 18 by 20 foot waterproof canvas sheet, a truck cover, always a useful thing, and later to prove of the very greatest value to us.

Another item of camp equipment peculiar to Australia and worthy of mention is the Bedourie camp oven, a flat round pressed-steel oven, light and unbreakable, which can be used for almost any sort of cooking — bread making, roasting or frying. The lid has separate hinged handles and makes an excellent frying pan. It is a tremendous improvement on the old cast-iron camp oven with its unnecessary legs. The meat boilers and billies are half-round for convenience of stowing in saddle bags, and all fit together in a nest. They boil very quickly with the flat side to the fire.

Rations were to last nine men for six weeks. The chief items were five fifty-pound bags of flour, and two hundred and fifty pounds of salt meat to be picked up at Andado Station. The meat was supplemented by several cases of "Imperial" assorted canned meats, a gift from Wm. Angliss (Aust.) Pty. Ltd., which were not only a luxury but later the only meat we had. Onions, potatoes, dried fruits, bacon, honey, golden syrup, rice, condensed milk, tea, coffee, cocoa, sugar, jam, cornflour, and as it was winter, 24 lb. of fresh butter, were included, and even curry powder, herbs and sauces were demanded by our professional cook. Some of these things I thought unnecessary at the time, but their bulk was small and when we had a day in camp, due to the rain or the place meriting a halt for scientific work, then Albert came into his own and we lived like kings, or at least better than some desert kings I have known. I long ago realized the sense and value of putting a small pillow in one's swag (this head-on-the-saddle stuff went out with the early Egyptians and persists only in novels), and after this experience I regard a cook as the next best thing to take.

To get information about Central Australia all you need do is to pay occasional visits to the "Black Bull" in Hindley Street, Adelaide, There you will meet in due course all the cattle men from the Centre, particularly during a good season, for the occasions, too few and far between, when there are cattle fit for the market and cheques are coming in, are always the family holiday times, and the "Black Bull" is the Mecca of these far-scattered people. If they are not staying there, they will forgather there, for it is the recognized rendezvous. The hotel is flanked with little shops displaying stock-whips and saddlery, and big hats and coloured shirts and riding boots. Here I found Bob McDill, owner of Andado Station, and was able with his help to make all plans for the early stages of the expedition without a preliminary visit to the starting point. Andado is well inside the western edge of the desert and no one knew conditions in the neighbourhood better than McDill. I thought he might like to come with us across the desert but he refused the invitation. His assistant on the station, Fred Sharpe, was equally well acquainted with the country and was most willing and anxious to come, but as he was undergoing serious medical treatment the risk of including him in the party was too great. McDill told me that they collected their mail from Abminga, on the railway line, which was about ninety miles from the homestead. A track ran from Abminga through Charlotte Waters on the telegraph line, across the Finke to Andado, with no difficulties except a couple of sandridges to be crossed near the station. Motor vehicles had got through, though they did not have any motor transport themselves. Stony country ran another 25 miles northward from the station tq Andado Bore No. 1, where water was obtainable, and a motor truck could get that far. From there northward and eastward only camels could be used owing to the sandridges.

McDill would supply us with meat if he had enough notice, but he had no blackboy suitable to accompany us. It was most important to take a native, the wilder the better. He would not be required or expected to know the country, but I knew the value of the natives on trips such as these, real bush natives who know the habits of all the bush creatures and can track and catch them. They are of the greatest help to the biologist and botanist in collecting, not to mention their well-known ability in tracking strayed camels or recovering any little article of camp equipment that is dropped or lost. A good bush native can be more valuable than any other single member of such an expedition. I have never forgotten how once in former days I lost a hammer off a gun while out shooting, and a native later followed my tracks and found it. I was staggered at the hopelessness of the quest, but even more that he expected to find it.

McDill knew of a boy, then with MacKinnon, the policeman at the Finke, but correspondence with MacKinnon disclosed that this boy had gone bush again. At one stage the blackboy was the only deficiency in the planning, and a serious one.

It was finally arranged that Jack Bejah should take the camels, with what loading was then ready, from Marree to Charlotte Waters, nearly four hundred miles, and the rest of the party should go by rail to Abminga and thence by motor truck to meet Jack and the camels at Charlotte Waters, where the whole party would assemble and the rest of the camel loads would be made up. The scientific staff would then go on by truck to Andado Station, followed by the camel string on its way to Andado Bore No. 1, where the truck would be left behind and the whole expedition would proceed by camel.

There was a great advantage in this long trip by the camels to the starting point. It was very necessary that all the camels should be in good training and working trim, and this journey would ensure it and allow the team to settle down and any weaknesses to be discovered while it was still possible to remedy them. However reliable Jack Bejah might be, it was a sound policy. Our whole success depended on our camels and their equipment, and that was my first care.

Harry Ding was to supply a motor truck and driver, to go up on the same train as the scientific staff. In Jack Bejah and Tom Kruse it was felt that we had the best camel man and the best outback motor driver the country could provide, and time proved that our confidence in them was justified.

The party leaving Adelaide Left to right: H. O. Fletcher, R. L. Crocker, C. T. Madigan, R. A. Simpson, D. Marshall, A. Hubbard.

In the bed of the Finke Near Charlotte Waters on the track to Andado.

4

WE GET AWAY

JACK BEJAH with the camels left Marree early in August for Charlotte Waters. He had been left to choose an assistant and he took a young Afghan, Nurie, and also a blackboy named Andy. He said he thought Andy would come all the way with us, and would be suitable. I left the decision on this till I had seen Andy and whatever other natives McKinnon or McDill might have when we arrived in their vicinity.

The rest of us, Crocker, Fletcher, Simpson, Marshall, Albert Hubbard and myself, left Adelaide by train on May 25th, 1939. It had been arranged with the Australian Broadcasting Commission that an attempt would be made to broadcast three talks from the desert. Colonel Thomas, then manager for the Australian Broadcasting Commission in Adelaide, had charge of the arrangements, and he came with us to Andado to see us safely on our way and to acquire some desert "atmosphere".

Tom Kruse joined the train in the night at Hawker, with his truck. He had driven across from Yunta. The train, the usual mixed one, was fully booked up and there was no sleeping accommodation for Tom-not that that was much worry to him. He slept as usual on the seat of his vehicle, which was on a railway wagon. He had no ticket, but the railways later prized a fare for him out of the expedition, raising a rather nice point over which we differed, my argument being that you pay for a seat on a train, theirs that you can't travel on a train without a ticket, which is not true; it is often done on those mixed trains.

At Marree old Bejah visited me on the train at six o'clock in the morning and told me that Jack had got away with all the gear in good order. He was obviously very pleased with the equipment and camels. He was very anxious to impress on me that we should never let the camels loose.

"Always have your camel in your hand" he kept repeating, shaking his hand as though holding a nose-line. It was not clear just how the camels were to get any feed. Bejah had had trouble with the camels getting away in the night during the Calvert Expedition, a thing that could be fatal.

At Mt. Dutton I saw my old companion of the Lake Eyre adventure, Charlie Kunoth, who was cooking for the railway gang. He gave us enormous mugs of tea and wished us luck.

Fred Wilkinson at Oodnadatta had seen Jack pass through with the camels, which they had photographed. It was not long ago, he said, that they used to photograph aeroplanes, but now there was one plane a day each way at Oodnadatta and the camel was something to turn out and see.

There had been heavy rains all along the railway line, and local pastoralists said they had never seen anything like the feed. This was a good augury for the desert. There had been several washaways on the railway, and trains were only just· getting through again. This was the first train that had run to schedule since the floods.

We arrived at Abminga at four o'clock in the morning of May 27th, in the dark and cold, and proceeded to off-load our truck and stores by the light of inadequate hurricane lamps. Fortunately there was a loading ramp there, but it was not easy to get the truck off sideways in the dark.

When the train had gone we found several men standing round a fire, and joined them till daylight should make it easier to load the truck and allow the moving picture camera to film the departure from Abminga, which place consisted of a little shed and a ramp, a fettlers' camp, a railway water tank and a notice board with the name in huge letters, all set in a featureless gibber plain.

At the fire were Fred Sharpe from Andado, in for the mail, and Lowe of Dalhousie, among several others. Fred told us that Jack was at the Charlotte with the camels, waiting for us. Lowe was one of the chief figures in the recent extraordinary affair of the supposed Leichhardt remains discovery, where a party went out to investigate what was said to be seven human skeletons lying round a camp fire in the sand ridges near Muckarinna waterhole on the Finke, forty miles east of Abminga. The skeletons proved to be merely calcified plant roots and bore little resemblance to human bones. Whether it was a hoax or a jest that was never intended to be taken seriously, was never determined, but the story originated in the "Black Bull," where newspaper reporters picked it up and started a snowball which ended in the State Government financing a so-called Leichhardt Expedition into the Simpson Desert. There had been one of the periodic references in the daily press to the disappearance of Leichhardt, including mention that the party consisted of seven men, and no doubt the reporters went to the "Black Bull" to get a little local colour for an article on Leichhardt. They would get it alright. There would be sure to be some men there from the wide open spaces who over a few drinks would tell more about Leichhardt than what there really is, like Punch's lighthouse keeper, and it is highly probable that this is what happened.

Before long an elaborate party was organized to penetrate the Simpson Desert on this interesting quest. It included an anthropologist, a moving picture photographer and a Government Surveyor, and was provided with seven coffins to bring back "the remains in. The Lowes took the party by truck to the site, which was on their country only a couple of hours run from the railway at Abminga, and showed them the petrified roots lying about over a considerable area. They said the bones had been scattered by cattle since they last saw them. Some of the party were for immediate return, but others thought they would at least use the anthropologist's sieves that they had brought, so they marked out a hundred and two ten foot squares and proceeded systematically to sieve the first six inches of the sand. Human tooth fragments, small fragments of bone, some of it human, and pieces of leather and iron turned up, which was surprising enough, but what was absolutely staggering was the discovery of two coins, a half sovereign dated 1817 and a threepenny bit dated 1841! The half sovereign on examination was seen to have been used as a pendant, probably a watch chain pendant, from the wear and the marks showing where it had been attached.

It was one of the first issues of half sovereigns, of which only a little over a million were minted. But this was nothing to the threepenny bit, which proved to be a Maundy threepence of which only 2,904 were minted in that year. It seems incredible that a coin so comparatively rare should be sieved out of the sand of the Simpson Desert. There was no sign saying "Dig," nothing to differentiate this spot from a million others on the sandridges. Leichhardt's last expedition started out in 1848, so the coins could have belonged to him or one of his party. One complete tooth built up of fragments. had the characteristics of a blackfellow's tooth. The bone fragments might of course have been of black man or white. It seemed most probable that the site was an old black's camp, as indeed almost every inch of the country within reach of a water-hole must have been at one time or other. Blacks would camp away while whites were on the water, and they would pick up or steal many little things. The leather, the iron and the coins might have come from any travellers such as exploring, telegraph construction or cattle-mustering parties, or from a neighbouring station, through the years subsequent to 1841. There is nothing to connect them with Leichhardt except remote possibility. The mystery of the coins is baffling and intriguing. It will probably never be solved. It seems to be a question of which is the more improbable, that the rare coins were actually lost there and the party had the extraordinary luck to dig for them on the very spot, or that the coins were planted, involving the planter having to get them somewhere at fairly short notice. Planting would seem more likely if it were not for the presence of the other relics indicating a camp site. The "Black Bull" and the Lowes are now inclined to be reticent on the subject. The story shows the value of reconnaissance, which could have been carried out by one man without any equipment in. a few days.

We got some bread and meat from the fettlers' camp at Abminga to see us through till our own stores and cooking gear were unpacked. Soon after sunrise all was loaded up and we left in the truck for the old telegraph station at Charlotte Waters, sixteen miles away across the gibber plains. The telegraph station, a group of well-made stone buildings, once a relay station and a busy centre, had long been closed. It had the forlorn and desolate aspect of all deserted places. From a telegraph station it had become a police station, and now even the police had left. It had been built almost as a fort and there were loopholes in the thick walls at the main door. I had been there twelve years before, when the place was still cheerfully occupied, but now an air of gloom and tragedy and decay seemed to surround it, and this was no mere fancy, for inside we found, in one room, the belongings of an old man who had been living there and had been dead for some time before he was discovered by Fred Sharpe a few days before. Fred and the police had removed the remains on a sheet of iron and buried them nearby; they had thrown sand on the floor, but it was still impossible to linger in the house.

The old telegraph buildings and an artesian bore with windmill and tanks half a mile away are all that there is at Charlotte Waters. My companions, from their memory of the prominence given to Charlotte Waters on school maps and it will be found in all atlases - had imagined that it was a town, the capital of a thriving centre. We found its one inhabitant dead. There was a little grave nearby with some nice ironwork railings round it. This proved to be the last resting place of a blacksmith's dog of old telegraph station days.

Jack was camped in the open nearby. I had expected to use the old buildings, but this was impossible, and anyway it was better to take to life under the sky straight away. There was Jack, with Nurie, the blackfellow Andy and the camels, all in good trim. They had struck no trouble on the journey up, which had taken them about three weeks. We had brought by train most of the stores and at once set about "breaking bulk" and making them up into loads and filling the camel boxes, which last takes a little thought so that things wanted first will be on top. There is nothing more irritating than to find the thing you seek at the bottom of a box full of loose tins and parcels, except to find that it isn't there but at the top of another box.

Simpson set up the wireless aerial ready for the first try-out when night came, and others did some natural history collecting in the neighbourhood.

The telegraph construction parties had found water in the shallow holes in the small creek now called the Coglin, and these gave the name to Charlotte Waters. The holes are far from being permanent, but at the time of our visit they were well filled and even contained little fish of which we took specimens. They were easily netted in the shallow water. One was later placed in a new genus, *Madigania*, but there was some question as to whether it deserved this treatment. There were actually ducks on the water, and I shot two, which we cooked that evening. The party felt that the proper thing to do was to cook them encased in mud in the coals, the supposed blackfellow method. It may be a native way, perhaps on the Murray, but I have never seen it used. It is usually hard to find any mud in Central Australia, and all flesh is simply put in the coals till it is slightly burnt on the outside but never cooked inside. It is merely warmed and singed by these inland natives. However, everyone knows of the excellence of duck cooked in a mud case, but few I imagine, have ever tried it. It is like that other myth, that when the boomerang misses its mark it returns to the thrower. The returning boomerang is a thin little thing, actually a toy, known only to a few tribes in the south. To make it return, the thrower must have a fresh breeze on his left hand. The hunting or fighting boomerang is quite a different thing, much heavier and stronger, with no returning properties. You will not find a returning boomerang among all the wild tribes of to-day. They have never heard of it. The mission blacks of the south are taught to make them for tourists. I have followed up the boomerang question and collected many boomerangs, but the only returning ones I have came from the Point McLeay Mission Station on the lower Murray, and from Ooldea on the east-west railway where they are being sold to the passengers. They are a fascinating toy, but the limitations of direction and manner of throwing make their returning properties of no practical value.

A friend of mine once said he was sure he had a good returning boomerang and asked me to test it, so we went outside and threw it in the approved manner. It travelled extraordinarily well, and was last seen passing over the roofs of some houses on the far side of a vacant block of land; we never saw it again, and decided it was not the returning kind.

I do not speak with authority on mud-cooking. It may have been general in the south, but I feel that it has been overrated and is a practice not likely to gain ground; in fact I am strongly in favour of letting it die out. The birds are not plucked, and in theory the feathers and skin come off with the clay when the savoury ball is cracked open. In the best practice I understand the entrails are left in, thus improving the cooking and preserving the flavour. I am not sure whether we observed this rule. Its omission may have been our undoing. Anyway it was not a success. It was practically raw, though Andy seemed to think it overdone if anything. There was plenty of good gamey flavour, but somehow not quite what one expected. A longer and slower baking was probably needed. One by one we quietly passed our portion on to Andy. Albert was disappointed at the results of his first effort to cook us a dinner. He had obviously not attended an aboriginal school of cookery, or perhaps the fault lay in our not being aborigines. Andy had no complaints, not even from over-eating.

That night Simpson made contact with Harry Ding at Yunta without any trouble, and we sent our first messages to the Australian Broadcasting Commission and *The Advertiser* newspaper to say that the whole expedition was assembled and looking forward to the desert trek.

The maximum temperature for the day was 76° F., and at night it fell to six degrees above freezing. Later we had colder days, and night temperatures below freezing. In spite of winter weather the flies were swarming at Charlotte Waters and Andado Station, making it difficult to eat or handle food. Out in the desert they disappeared. Human occupation encourages them; stock manure is their chief breeding ground.

Fred Sharpe arrived at the camp during the morning and spent the night with us. His transport was a very unusual camel buggy, an old Ford car minus the engine, drawn by a pair of camels and followed by several spare animals attached behind. It was an excellent thing for crossing sandridges and he could make the journey of eighty miles from Abminga to Andado in a day of non-stop travelling. It was a great sight to see it in action, with Fred at the steering wheel and the spare parts following behind.

Before we turned in, all the camel loads were made up and all gear checked. Everything was there; nothing was forgotten; men, material and transport, all were assembled, and the party lay down to sleep on the ground in the first camp, cheerful and full of anticipation of the adventure ahead.

5

ANDADO STATION

By ten o'clock next day, a Sunday, the camel string was loaded and we started it off on the sixty-five mile journey to Andado Station, preceded by the camel buggy. The scientific staff with their personal gear boarded the truck and shot on ahead. It was a three-day journey for the camels and we intended to wait for them at Andado, where time could be usefully spent in making future plans and examining the edge of the desert.

The track from Charlotte Waters to Andado runs east along the Coglin Creek to the Finke, which is crossed near the Coglin junction. It follows the left bank of the Finke for a few miles before turning north into the desert towards Mt. Peebles. After the Finke is left the track runs for about eighteen miles between sandridges till it reaches a stony patch free from sandridges, an area about thirty miles long east and west by twelve miles wide. There are several conspicuous hills in this area, notably Mt. Peebles, a "trig." station, and Mt. Day behind it, with the Moolta Tableland at the east end. The track passes close to the east of Mt. Peebles and near Mt. Day it turns north-east to run straight to the Station past the north end of the Moolta Tableland.

The Finke at the crossing was a wide valley full of gum trees and high grasses. It is under water only when the river is in flood, which is by no means every year. There was actually only one defined channel to cross, a deep, narrow and dry ditch. Owing to recent rains the vegetation was profuse. Particularly conspicuous was the plant locally called verbena that grew in dense thickets several feet high in the lower ground along the edges of waterholes, which were then dry, and a vine called by the natives *ilkarta*, that twined among the lower shrubs and was covered with little green melons the size of large gooseberries, very popular with the natives and quite pleasant to eat. Some of the grasses were head high.

About seven miles from the river and among the sandridges we came upon Mayfield's Swamp which was then a big sheet of shallow water, a large claypan. No streams appeared to enter it, and it was rather surprising to· see so much water. It was the only surface water we found between the water-holes in the Coglin and the claypans in the centre of the desert. There were no signs of water in the Finke Valley, in fact a newcomer could have crossed the Finke at that point without recognizing it as a river at all.

Andado Station lies off the stony area and in the edge of the sandridge desert. Two high sandridges have to be crossed to reach it. The first one is the more difficult, and one wondered if our truck would ever manage it. We inspected it first. It was about fifty feet high, with the usual comparatively gentle rise of sand fixed by spinifex on the western side and a nasty ridge of live sand on the top, but without any abrupt faces. Kruse charged it at full speed from several hundred yards away, wildly and recklessly, but just failed to reach the top. He decided to back down and charge again. He carried two eighteen foot lengths of three inch water piping, which is much the best thing for getting vehicles out of either sand or mud, and makes matting or wire quite unnecesssary, but it can only be used if the vehicle has dual rear wheels. The end of the piping is thrust in between the two tyres from behind or in front, depending on which way you want to go, and the pipes may be left sticking up in the air. When the clutch is let in the tyres grip the piping and draw it under, and the vehicle will run along the pipes and out of the worst of bogs. It is a very quick and rapid method of backing out of mud bogs, as we saw later on the Diamantina. In the case of mud, to back out and try somewhere else is always the best thing to do. Going forward in sand presents less difficulties than in mud as the pipes are drawn inwards through the sand as the vehicle advances. They cannot be put under the front wheels as well as the back so they are not parallel when the vehicle starts. A heavy load becomes an advantage rather than a disadvantage. It is pipes that get the Birdsville mail through in wet weather. With single tyres the pipes are useless, and the difficulties of bogs are much greater. The term bog is used for both sand and mud in the back country.

At the second charge our truck reached the summit, and on starting again on the pipes it succeeded in running down the far side. The track then ran between two sandridges for a couple of miles to where there was a lower crossing of the next sandridge and a sandy way into the valley in which the station lay. Here we found a typical Central Australian cattle station homestead, a corrugated iron house nicely white-washed, some gum trees, well-built stockyards, and a well and windmill nearby, with the usual blacks' camp in the offing, all walled in between two high red sandridges that stretched as far as the eye could see. Everything looked very arid and there was no feed to be seen round the station.

Bob McDill was away, but we were met by his assistants, Mr. and Mrs. Brooks, with Fred Sharpe and his mate Lady and their little daughter Storm, and also a boy called Wal. Lady and Fred cooked a turkey Marshall had shot on the way out, and we all had an excellent dinner. Fred had left his camel buggy to his native assistants and had come on with us on the truck as guide. We made a stack of our gear and the sand began to pile up over it. That night we had to sleep on the ground outside, and this is never very pleasant when close to a homestead. The wind eddied round and the sand poured over us, and with fowls and goats about it is not always all sand. A tame magpie came picking at our faces at the crack of dawn. It visited us all and each tried to persuade it to go to his neighbour.

In the morning everyone got into his desert dress, and all superfluous gear and clothing was sorted out for return to Marree, where it would await us at the close of the expedition. Col. Thomas had to return to Adelaide, so I went back to Abminga with him in the truck and left the surplus luggage there for railing to Marree. We were sorry to say good-bye to Col. Thomas, who had been a very cheerful and interesting companion. On the return I camped for the night at the Finke and next morning examined the edge of the tableland round which the river flows before turning south. It is only about a hundred feet high. On the top we found a curious arrangement of stones in the form of a sort of yard, over sixty yards long and twenty feet wide. Inside the yard there were many stone slabs turned up on edge without definite arrangement. It must have been the work of the aboriginals but its significance was obscure. It suggested an imitation stockyard.

The camels reached Andado that afternoon. Jack was disappointed at the lack of feed, and took them several miles up the valley to find fodder. McDill turned up with pack horses the same evening.

That night I took astronomical observations for the position of the station, after comparing the chronometer with the wireless time signals, which came through clearly at seven o'clock each night. The station was not marked on any maps.

Next day we brought in all the camel canteens and filled them with water from the Andado Well. It was excellent water. Most of the party then made a picnic trip to a well three miles to the west, to dig for marsupial mice and to bring in a load of wood. They had no luck with the digging so Fletcher returned with the truck to set traps for the night. He was so long gone that we thought the party was lost in the sandridges, so we lit a fire on the high ridge to the west to guide them in, which seemed rather to have annoyed them. They had been doing some more digging and this time they had succeeded in catching some mice.

While they were out there they had been questioning Lady on the art of tracking and she had given a demonstration. She found two dingo tracks going away from the well, and said one of the dogs was poisoned. She showed them where it had suffered fits. Later Brooks found a dead dog not far from the well.

That evening we had a mishap with the wireless. All three transmission valves blew out, for no known reason, and this left us without any spares. We made arrangements for more spares to be sent to Oodnadatta by plane and then on to Abminga by rail. This accident was disconcerting, particularly as the cause remained undiscovered. It kept us another three days at Andado, but the time was well spent.

The following day we went out by truck to Andado Bore No.1, twenty-five miles northward of the station. On the way we passed Jack Bejah and the camels, with Andy and Nurie. When Jack first looked round Andado he said rather gloomily that it was a desolate place and that he would get poking on, an expression he always used for moving with the camels I never agreed with his apologetic attitude towards his means of transport. It may be slow, but it gets you there. It has the advantage of dependability, and in places where camels go men are not the slaves of time.

We had now discovered that the heavy rains had missed Andado, where only a couple of inches had fallen in the past six months, and that had been swallowed up by the sand. Stock feed was very low, and Jack was rather worried. It was arranged that he should poke along a few miles each day searching for feed, and arrive at the bore in three days' time. We wanted to start the heavy sandridge work with the camels in the best possible condition.

The track from the station to the bore lay for the first ten miles between the two station sandridges; then the eastern sandridge gave out and we rounded its end. We were then on stony flats against which all the desert sandridges came to an end. We rounded the ends of four of them as we passed along this edge of the desert, and arrived at the bore in twenty-five miles.

We found later that this second stony tableland extended north-east for about twenty-five miles in a narrow tongue to the Todd-Hale junction. As far as we could ascertain it did not connect up with the Mt. Peebles stony tract, but the two of them form a more or less sandridge-free peninsula extending into the desert from the Finke. The main Simpson Desert lies to the east of the peninsula, with the Depot Sandhills, through the western edge of which the railway runs, making a big bay to the west.

The bore had been sunk to a depth of 870 feet and the water stood at seventy feet below the surface. Most of the Simpson Desert lies on the Great Artesian Basin but the bores do not flow near its margin, which runs from Charlotte Waters in a north-easterly direction across to the Queensland border, with the basin to the south of this line. The windmill and tanks were but of action but there was a windlass and "sand-pump", a long tube with a valve in the bottom, by means of which water could be raised. Near the bore there was a patch of "waddy" trees, tall, straight trees some fifty feet high, with thin and drooping foliage and seeds in long pods. The wood is red and very hard and heavy, a perfect timber for blackfellows' waddies. The tree is an acacia, *Acacia peuce*. There are only two known localities for this tree in Australia, the Andado bore grove and another a few miles north of Birdsville. It is known as "waddy" at Birdsville and casuarina at Andado. It has a resemblance to the sheoak or casuarina in shape and foliage but the seeding habit is quite different. The she oak bears cones or "apples" while the waddy seeds are in pods. Like the isolated *Livistona mariae* palms near Hermannsburg, it probably once had a much wider distribution.

We brought a load of posts in from the bore for McDill, who went out with us. One hoped that a few waddy trees would be allowed to survive.

We caught a small yellow rabbit at the bore, and took it back as a pet for Storm. It had run into a length of bore casing. We later saw a few more rabbits on the Hale further north, but not another sign of them in the whole desert crossing and beyond, until we reached the Diamantina River far below Birdsville. Drought had driven them out of this part of the country, but they reappear in good seasons with astonishing rapidity. It is unlikely that they ever populate the Simpson Desert itself.

Between the station and the bore we caught some desert mice, and dug out a scorpion. The scorpion burrows down in a spiral several feet in diameter, so that a hole dug inside the spiral exposes the burrow coiling round it, with the scorpion at the end.

A bullock had been killed at the station and the meat was now ready for us. In this country the meat is not corned in a brine tub, but the salt is rubbed into it by hand and the pieces are then hung up for a couple of days to drip and dry. On trek it is spread out each night on branches of trees broken down for the purpose, till it is quite dry on the surface, when it can be left in the bags and will keep for months in the summer and almost indefinitely in winter. If dingoes are about it has to be hung up in the trees till it is dry - a laborious job.

We had now got all the information that Bob McDill, Fred Sharpe and the natives could give us on the surrounding country, and it was clear that the original plan to go up to the Todd-Hale junction and cross due east to the Mulligan River needed no modification, but would best achieve our object.

The Hale is known to aboriginals as the Allitera, which name was always used at Andado. About six miles up the Allitera from its junction with the Todd we were told there was a native soak called Allua, and we decided to go to this for a final fill up with water before turning east. The soak was about sixty miles from the station. An old aboriginal, Ly-Ly, would come with us from Andado to show us the soak, and then return by himself to the station.

By this time I had seen enough of Andy to decide that he would do as a member of the expedition. He was extraordinarily keen and energetic for an aboriginal, and had already shown his enthusiasm for collecting. Ly-Ly was too old, and there was no other suitable aboriginal on the station, nor had Constable McKinnon been able to produce one. The only catch was that

Andy was rather hesitant about going. He obviously feared the desert, but Jack Bejah managed to overcome his fears. He had been brought up on the Killalpaninna Mission on the Birdsville track and knew the south side of the desert. The Mission was long closed and the remains of Andy's people, the Dieri, had drifted into Marree. Andy was about middle-aged. He spoke quite fair English, and even knew some German words and phrases, which always seemed utterly incongruous. My opinion of him improved daily and he turned out to be one of the highlights of the expedition.

Other information obtained from McDill was that both the Todd and Allitera had only a single channel above the junction, not the wide belt of braided channels commonly shown on maps, and that they flooded out at the junction to four miles wide without definite channels, and continued so for some ten miles, when a single channel was again formed running to the latitude of Andado, another forty miles, where there was a swamp about thirty-five miles east of the station, below which the river continued in numerous ill-defined channels between the sandridges. He also told of a round hill called Poodnitera, near the junction, a conspicuous landmark.

The next day the truck went into Abminga for the spare valves and more petrol, taking McDill and Sharpe. Crocker and Fletcher were to go to the Finke and remain there to do some collecting, but the whole party went on into Abminga and played cards at the fettlers' camp, of which I took a very poor view, particularly later when I heard of the money supposed to have been won from me in the camp. It made a good story, to have taken the leader of the expedition down at poker.

They saw Ted Colson at Abminga, in for the mail from his home at Blood's Creek. He was sorry he had missed the party when we all arrived by the previous mail. He had been rather late and we had got away early. He sent a message generously wishing us luck, though he must have envied us the staff and equipment that he so sadly lacked for the expedition he had to abandon.

Marshall and I did some photography round the station while the rest were away and then ran a section across several sandridges to the east of the station. The first sandridge to the east was one of the largest in the whole desert. It was 84 feet high, with a big crest of live sand in dunes and mounds on top. The steep faces of the crest were quite difficult to climb owing to the sand giving way and sliding down. Like nearly all the desert sand, it was a bright red and responded well to colour photography.

The little girl Storm spent the afternoon with us. Her magpie rather interfered with the instrument work by alighting on heads at unexpected moments; she was in the habit of going round with it on her own head. After a while she got tired of watching us and wandered off. One of her proudest possessions was a pair of sun spectacles and during the afternoon she lost them somewhere in the sand. She had covered a good mile of country in her wanderings, and after half an hour I gave up the search as hopeless. When Lady heard of this she at once went out, followed all the wandering tracks unerringly, and was soon back with the glasses. Like the man with the gun-hammer, it was not a matter of looking for them; she just went out and got them.

We were no doubt a highlight in Storm's life, but she was of almost as much interest to us and her quaint sayings were a continual amusement. She referred to Simpson, who wore puttees, as the man with the tape round his legs. When she found we were interested in the native names of things she was very proud to tell them to us, and was always saying "You ask me that one". While at the station we got the meaning of most of the better-known local place names. To give a few examples: *Andado* means stone-knife; *Abmiriga,* snake's track; *Rodinga*, road or foot; and *Rumbalara*, rainbow. The Andado swamp is called *Ajajacun,* literally "meat inside". *Apma* is the snake, *elunja* the galah, *angala* the crow, and *errkuppa* the waddy tree.

One day Marshall got some good colour film of clearing sand from the stockyard by horse scoop, a frequent necessity if the yard is to be prevented from becoming a solid heap of sand. The open structure of railings seems more effective in accumulating sand-drift than a solid building like a house. I have seen the stockyards at Parachilna Railway Station in front of the Flinders Ranges in South Australia so drifted-up that stock could walk over the top of them, and part of the fence and the railway yard gate completely buried, yet the offices and houses were quite free of sand. Buildings cause eddies in the wind which scour the sand away rather than build it up.

On the afternoon of Sunday, June 4th, a week after our arrival, we left Andado in the truck for the bore, taking the filled canteens, the meat, and the members' personal gear. On the way we stopped to catch a few more marsupial mice. At the bore we found Jack, Nurie and Andy with the camels and stores waiting for us. They had found some good feed ten miles short of the bore and had stopped there, coming on to the bore only that day. That night I observed for the position of the bore, which was only very approximately placed on the map. Crocker acted as recorder for the astronomical observations throughout, and was very efficient at it, reading the chronometer like an old hand.

We were all together that night, eager to get into camel marching order next day and start the real desert trek as a single unit.

The edge of the desert *Acacia peuce* on the stony plain at Andado Bore No. I. This tree is known only in two small patches, this one and another near Birdsville.

6
NORTHWARD TO THE HALE

THE truck was to leave us here at the bore, so it was now neces¬sary to make everything up into camel loads. The seven camels were already detailed for their fourteen water canteens, and the provisions had been distributed at Charlotte Waters, but the personal gear and scientific equipment still remained to be loaded on. The proper making up of camel loads is of fundamental importance and is quite a technical business. With poor loading there is not only the danger of losing things, but there will be continual delay in adjusting loads. Then again, some things will not be used perhaps for weeks, while others may be wanted several times during a day's march, so there must be an order of priority and accessibility. The wanted things like firearms, cameras, collecting bottles and other scientific gear must be securely fastened yet easily detached. Much experience is necessary for complete success, and usually one is making improvement thoughout the whole journey.

The riding camels were allotted to the riders, and each had to make up his own load of blankets and personal gear, and such instruments as he might want during the march. Fletcher required an extra camel for his collecting bottles and spirit cans, but Marshall managed to get his photographic equipment on to his own riding camel. Simpson's wireless gear made up the best part of another camel load, and then there were the theodolite, chronometer, plane table, thermometers and other small gear to find a place for. The leather pack-bags for riding saddles and the extra wooden tucker boxes lent by the Police simplified the loading considerably.

It is essential to have some containers and not to try to tie everything on to the camels in bundles, as the Arabs do. I once saw some Italian mica miners in the Hart Ranges who had every article dangling on strings from their camels, including hurricane lamps and frying pans and coffee pots, after the style of Tenniel's White Knight.

To the newcomer the loading of camels is always a fearsome business. The camels roar and show their teeth in a most alarming manner.

Actually it is a groan rather than a roar, a protest far from mute but not belligerent, in fact merely an inherited habit that means nothing. The old camel-hand takes no notice of it at all, and in a few days even the beginner finds himself so used to it as to be quite unconscious of the noise. Once the load is on, the camel makes no further sound till next loading time, not even a grunt of satisfaction when the load is taken off.

We decided to give the camels a drink, as it might be their last for a month if the Allua soak failed us, so we got the sand-pump going. Winding this up by windlass was so slow that most of the water had leaked out of the tube by the time it reached the surface, but the enterprising Tom Kruse soon altered this. He detached the end of the wire rope from the windlass and fixed it to the rear of his truck, leaving a few turns on the windlass, and then went ahead with the truck, thus making a sort of miners' "whip" with the truck instead of a horse. The windlass looked as if it would fly to pieces at any moment as it whirled round, but the tube shot up practically full and the camels were soon watered at the trough. The water was not very good. In addition to its natural high mineral content, it had been long standing in the casing and was rather black and odoriferous. However, the camels drank it, and we topped up the partially-used canteens with it.

At last everything was loaded up, we mounted the riding camels, and the procession moved off. I led the way on Snowy, Jack's riding camel, closely followed by Albert on his young beast, over which he never succeeded in exercising any control; it just followed me round like a dog. Then came the rest of the riding camels followed by Jack Bejah walking and leading the string of baggage camels.

Jack said he was going to walk across the Simpson Desert, but his dog had no such ambition. It sat between the big tucker boxes for the whole journey, only getting off when the camel knelt down. Nurie and Andy brought up the rear on foot. Later on when the loads had lightened, everyone could ride who wanted.

The truck started up and we waved a farewell to Tom Kruse as he turned back for Andado and the railway.

Ly-Ly had joined us at the bore, complete with camel and equipment, which was all apparently his own. He was an aboriginal of some importance, and a property owner. He knew little English and was very reticent, and an old man. I found it very difficult to get any information out of him, which was not due to any unwillingness on his part but to my lack of understanding.

Andy had very quickly assumed the role of collector. He needed no prodding. It was a job right into his hands, and old Ly-Ly soon took the cue and became equally enthusiastic. A spirit of competition developed between them in catching lizards, snakes and mice.

It was early afternoon when we started off on a north-east course towards the Todd-Hale junction. In six miles we were off the stony ground round the bore, and entered low sandridges. After crossing them for an hour we halted and made the first desert camp, eight miles from the bore, with ten sandridges behind us and a thousand before. It was a very barren camp, in spinifex and dead mulga. Not a living tree was to be seen.

In six miles next morning, after crossing another 28 small sandridges, we were again on a grassy plain with a broken tableland on our right. It appeared that we had merely crossed a sandy bay on the west side of the higher ground. Near the end of the tableland we sighted a little round outlying hill which I took to be Poodnitera, and we made for it and camped there, rather early in the afternoon.

Like all hills in very flat country, the tableland looked imposing, but proved to be only sixty feet high. It was quite narrow here and ended in a point. It was composed of a porcelainized shale, very similar to the formations at the Finke River, but was here capped by a pebbly conglomerate.

There were signs of recent rain along the tableland edge and there was plenty of camel feed at the camp, including green buck-bush, and the succulent munyeroo.

From the tableland we got a good view all round. A mile out in front of the end of the tableland. tongue there were two lone little twin hills close together. I was uncertain whether these twins were Poodnitera, or the single larger hill with a flat top on the west side of the tongue. To the north of the Twins there were irregular lines of small gum trees among sandridges, obviously flooded country, but no defined water channels could be seen. The patches of trees had a south-easterly trend and apparently marked the course of the Todd. A better-defined line of trees coming down from the north, and more to the east, marked the course of the Hale or Allitera. The lines met about three miles to the east of our position.

Next morning we reached the Twins in two miles and climbed the more northerly one, where we found a cairn of stones, possibly built by Day. We pulled it down to search for any message left there, but found none. We left one of our own in a tin and rebuilt the cairn. From the Twins the courses of the two rivers were clearer. A tableland edge on the east side of the Hale could be seen, about eight miles away, bearing 5°. I questioned Ly-Ly on the hill about his soak, but could get nothing definite. He had no idea of distances in miles, but he seemed to convey that the soak was where the tableland could be seen. This tallied with McDill's estimate of six miles above the junction of rivers, being rather more than less. Anyway, the next thing to do was to go to this point. There was a large dry claypan on the south-west side of the Twins, which Ly-Ly called Djibata. This name seemed to include the Twins as well.

In the first six miles north of the Twins we crossed thirty-eight close sandridges, most of them small but some up to fifty feet high. We crossed the Todd without noticing it. We would not have known it was there if it had not been for the view from the Twins, showing the extra vegetation between the sandridges. After six miles we entered green grassy flats and trees along the course of the Hale, and after two miles crossed its one well-defined channel and camped among trees between the channel and the low tableland edge sighted from the Twins. This was a delightful spot, with gidgee against the cliffs, and box and swamp gum and dense undergrowth on the river flats. The channel was little more than a ditch and it was obvious that in flood times it would overflow and cover a considerable width. There were flowing acacias and munyeroo on the sandridges between the rivers and high green flowering plants on the flooded areas among the trees along the Hale. There was plenty of firewood, and it was a perfect camping place, except for the lack of water. We were not to see its like again till we reached the Hay.

There was another cairn on the edge of the tableland at this camp. We searched again for any messages, but found nothing, so left one of our own. Cattle have been brought down this river from the MacDonnells from time to time and possibly the drovers had put these cairns up as landmarks. The natives often build them too, in imitation of the white man's trigonometrical stations, a thing to be remembered when searching for the trig. points of surveyors.

For the past two days we had seen budgerigars, which do not go far

"THE DOG SAT ON THE TUCKER BOX."

from water, and to-day there were zebra finches and pigeons as well. The tracks of emus and wild camels were noticed. There was a rabbit warren near the camp, with a few rabbits, the last we were to see of Brer Rabbit for the whole journey across the desert.

This was the place indicated by Ly-Ly from the top of the Twins, and it was more than McDill's six miles up from the junction, yet there were no signs of water, and no holes in the channel big enough to hold water for any length of time. In the deeper places the sand was damp and obviously water had not long dried up, but it was not suitable for a soakage; there was not enough sand, only a veneer on sandy clay, and no hard rock bottom. Next day Jack and I put down a twelve-foot hole in the best place, without success. The hole was mainly through clay, becoming drier as we went down. We carried a post-hole borer with which we could sink twenty feet, a tool with tremendous advantages over the shovel for water search.

I hoped to observe for position that night, in order to fix the Hale-Todd Junction, but the sky was overcast.

The following day was spent by the botanist and biologist in collecting, while Jack and I searched for water. There were plenty of spiders, scorpions and lizards, and Andy was very busy and keen. Marshall made a colour film of Andy getting a widgetty grub out of a gum tree and eating it. The presence of the grub in the tree can be detected by a bulge on the trunk the size of a cupped hand, with a hole just below it, marked by a red stain, out of which borings and excreta exude. The bulge is chopped into with an axe, disclosing a hole extending upwards. Into this the native pushes a stick or strong grass stem turned back at the end like the barb on a harpoon. When the stick is gently withdrawn the barb drags the grub down. The grubs are white and of the order of six inches long and half an inch in diameter, with a small brown head. The natives eat them raw or roasted on coals, holding them by the head and biting off the remainder. The body is mainly composed of a fatty substance and smells good when roasted.

Ly-Ly was the most difficult person to get information out of that I had ever met. I could not discover whether he expected to find the soak here or not. I began to think it was a long time since he had been here and he had forgotten the place, or that the soak might be a hundred miles away up in the MacDonnells. It was not absolutely essential to find water, but we had used four days' supply and I wanted to replenish this and leave for the desert crossing with a full load. At four o'clock on the day of our arrival Ly-Ly had disappeared on his camel, but turned up again at ten o'clock next morning saying he had found the soak. Of course I could not gather just where it was, so I sent Jack off with him on camels to investigate. Jack came back in the evening, saying the soak was there all right, seven miles upstream. He had taken a shovel and dug down to water. On this good news I decided to shift camp to the place next day.

Andy was in great form that night, even more cheerful than usual. He told us of an old man who had made the Georgina run by means of the rain ceremony, which takes a very big rain, and a big witch doctor too. Only the old men can do this, said Andy, good men; no drink, no cards. Fletcher asked him how they stopped it if it rained too much, but this need does not seem to have arisen. One gathered that Andy did not consider his own years and moral standing sufficient for rain making. He may have given it a surreptitious try-out, for it rained gently all night and gave our ground sheets a good testing, or rather the arranging of them.

There is nothing more unpleasant than having to break a camp after a wet night. One potters about hoping things will dry out, unwilling to roll up damp blankets, wondering what to do next, and generally wasting time. It was well after ten o'clock next day when at last we got on the move.

We first heard the yaps and mournful howls of the dingoes at this camp. They were heard almost every night afterwards and often seen peering over the crests of the sandridges down on to our camps, desert outcasts gazing in hungry loneliness on the feasts they longed to share.

We went northward between the river and the edge of the tableland, crossing sandy saltbush flats that made wide bays in the tableland, and soon covered the seven miles to the soakage. An emu was seen near the soak walking about rather suspiciously, and it was not long before some of the party found her nest with four eggs. The whole party breakfasted on the eggs next morning, one emu egg being enough for a meal for four men. Ly-Ly seemed rather annoyed about this. He had not helped to find the nest and the general idea was that he wanted to find it after we had gone, as this was where we were to part, his job of locating the soak being done. Apart from this little set-back, he was very excited. The locality was obviously an old native camping ground; probably a place for ceremonies, and he rushed round apparently locating spots of particular interest to him, or where he had camped in the old days when large gatherings took place there. . He said there was plenty of food about, "bloody widgetty, bloody yam, bloody mobs". He did not mention bloody emu eggs. Exactly fifty per cent of Ly-Ly's conversation consisted of bloody. He used it as a sort of prefix to every word and no doubt regarded it as an essential part of word structure. He reminded me of the story of the man who was asked by a friend what this one man one vote business meant. He answered, "Well, it's like this, you see, Fred; one bloody man, one bloody vote". "Oh, I see," said the friend, "why can't they explain it to you like that?"

I really saw yams for the first time at this camp, after hearing many erroneous descriptions of them by people who had not seen them. They are usually said to be like potatoes, to which they actually bear. no resemblance at all. They are the roots of a vine-like plant that has little foliage and is rather hard to find. It may be seen climbing on other low plants and brambles. The roots are cylindrical and may be several feet long and no thicker than your finger, with a dark skin, but fleshy inside. When collected for roasting they look like a bundle of thin sticks. They are cooked on the coals and taste rather like a tough and fibrous parsnip. There was a sandy bank near the camp where floods had washed away some soil, and the roots could be seen sticking out of it and were very easy to get. We all ate some, but they could only be looked on as an emergency diet.

Andy and Ly-Ly kept to themselves at this camp and prepared their own bush tucker. They had cooked a lot of widgetties and these attracted' Simpson and Crocker, who, though not anxious for a bush meal, wanted to try the widgetties. Ly-Ly had roasted the grubs in the ashes and laid them out on pieces of bark. Simpson and Crocker each ate four, and like Huck Finn, they could have eaten a lot more if they'd wanted to, but they didn't want to. They pulled the head and tail sections away and thus removed most of the digestive tract, a black string, and then drew out the inside of the grub from the dry and browned skin. Actually this is a much too refined and wasteful way of eating them. Only the hard head should be thrown away.

The Hale or Allitera here had a broad sandy bed fifty yards wide, but this was the end of it as a well-defined single channel. Beyond, it flooded out into swamps and ditches. The sand was saturated with water a few feet below the surface. All hands turned to and dug a large soak about six feet deep and twenty feet across, a big excavation owing to the caving of the sides. This always happens with sand soaks. You have to dig over a much bigger area than you think at first and it is almost impossible to get down more than a few inches below water level without timbering. The task made a good piece of colour film, the sand flying at an astonishing rate while the eye of the camera was on the workers. Troughs were made in the sand and lined with ground sheets for the camels to drink from.

The sky was clear that night and I was able to get star observations for position. I had to work these out and set the course for the morrow before turning in. "Mudloo Well" was marked on the maps, between the Queensland border and the Mulligan River. I had no information about this well, whether it was a permanent waterhole, a dug well, or even if it was still is existence, but it offered the nearest chance of water the other side of the desert and I decided to set my course for it. I found its magnetic bearing from our present position was only a degree north of east and its distance a hundred and fifty miles away by air line across the sandridge desert. Next morning we would start out on this course into the unknown, and the real task of the expedition would begin. We were then about sixty miles north of Andado Station.

A national broadcast, Hay River. *(l to r)* Madigan, Fletcher, Simpson, Crocker.

7
EASTWARD INTO THE DESERT

IN the morning we emptied out the bore water and topped up all the canteens with water from the soak. It was beautiful water, clear and soft, and had quite settled during the night after the disturbance of our excavations. The camels showed little interest in our beautiful white troughs and only a few would drink. Jack said the water was too cold for them. Owing to the weather and the green feed about along the river, this did not seem to matter much at the time.

It was nearly noon on Sunday, June 11, before we got away.

We had spread all our gear out in the sun to dry after the wetting of the night before. When all was ready we said farewell to Ly-Ly, who was going to spend a few days alone in his old haunts before returning to Andado, mounted our camels, turned our backs on the river and headed into the desert. The venture we had prepared for was begun.

We climbed a small gully to the top of the scarp, only about fifty feet high, that bordered the river, and found ourselves on a stony tableland that proved to be no more than a couple of miles across. Beyond it was a valley nearly three miles wide, with a watercourse in the bottom, running away south-south-east. This valley also had plenty of green feed in it, with gum trees, acacias and flocks of shell parrots or budgerigars. A slight rise on the other side of the valley again brought us to a stony tableland where there were a few small sandridges and some dry claypans. In lower areas there was green mulga and herbage, but everywhere the gum trees were dead, both box and bloodwood. There were patches where the dead timber and brushwood had been burnt. It is always a mystery how such fires start, though this burning might have been done by aborigines as we were not far from water. The vegetation, though dead, had been comparatively dense, dense enough to burn in places. We camped early on a green patch with a sandridge on the far side. There were zebra finches round the camp. We had made only eleven miles and crossed five sandridges, but it was a propitious beginning. There was some feed about, the camels were in good condition, all the equipment had been tested and found satisfactory, there was a ton of water on the camels, and everything was running smoothly. It was a good camp, and Albert made us an excellent dinner from tinned meats. In the morning the empty tins were fixed up in a mulga tree to attract the attention of the next comer, if he comes before the tins rust away. There is a fascination in finding in lonely places signs that others have passed that way: It made us go to the trouble of taking down and rebuilding the cairns on the Hale. I hope somebody some day sees those empty meat tins again. He will take them down and try to read the lettering on them and to figure out who left them there.

The temperature fell to two degrees below freezing that night, and the dingoes kept us awake with their howling.

It was midwinter and the days were short. The sun rose at about seven o'clock and set at five. The routine for the day's march was to rise at the first daylight, about half past six, breakfast, break camp, and start moving as soon as possible, and then to keep on the move till it was time to camp again, without any luncheon halt, with its inevitable unpacking of loads and loss of time. This also allowed the camels the maximum time for feeding after camp was made in the evening, for we took no chances with them at night but yarded them up as soon as it was dark. Jack made the most incredible yards with a single strand of rope round four corner sticks, using standing trees where there were any, or stakes that he carried when there were none. The camels were hobbled and herded inside this, where, to my astonishment, they stayed. It was only a token yard, but Jack said they would think it was the real thing, and apparently they did. Sometimes in the morning it would be found that one or two had rolled under the rope, but it did not seem to matter much which side of the line they were on, reminding one of the man going round the outside of the park railings and lamenting that he was locked in again.

Our object was to get on the move by 9 a.m., though this idea was rarely realized, and to camp about 4 p.m., thus allowing the camels about two hours to feed at night and perhaps an hour in the morning before we were ready to begin loading. Feed would have to be fairly plentiful for this to be enough time for them. In the early stages of the expedition we only had two meals a day ourselves while on the march, which was no hardship.

Off-loading a camel team at camp time is a quick process. The camels kneel down in their line, the slip knots on each load are pulled free and the cordage is paid out, allowing the two loads to slide gently to the ground, one on each side of the camel. One man can release the loads of the whole team in a few minutes. The pack saddles are then lifted off and placed on end at one side, the hobbles put on, nose-lines removed and the camel is free to go off and feed. Most of the loads can be left undisturbed, and when reloading time comes the camel is lead up and kneels down between his loads again; but it takes two men to put the loads on, one for each side. The loads have to be lifted together and held on the knees against the saddle while cordage is passed across from the top of one load to the other and secured. Jack and Albert always did this part of the loading. A competition in smartness and efficiency developed between them, and though Jack was much the bigger and stronger, Albert kept his end up right through the whole journey. Every morning Jack's cheery and' continued cries of "Come on, Albert", were a familiar feature of the packing up. Each rider, of course, packed his own camel.

As soon as we left the Hale it was arranged that water should be used only from the two four-gallon canteens; which were filled from the larger ones every morning before starting, and that quantity must last till next morning. This put the party of nine on a ration of eight gallons a day. The small canteens also had the advantage of being much easier to handle.

So far we had been on stony ground, with claypans, good feed in patches, and only a few straggly sandridges. What lay beyond the sandridge by the camp? Next morning we were soon across it; closely following came another, and then another, and another. Spinifex began to replace all other herbage. The trees disappeared. The sandridges became higher and straighter, and were soon up to fifty feet high. Camel feed was reduced to a few plants on the crests of the ridges. The country and the going became steadily worse. At the end of six and a half hours we had crossed no less than seventy sandridges in sixteen miles, and then camped among them in a place with little feed and only a few sticks of dead needlebush for firewood. We were into the desert. It was going to be tough.

At first there had been some stony patches, showing that the hard surface was not far below the sand, but now there was only sand and spinifex between the sandridges.

The following day was much the same. At noon we passed a tree-covered claypan between sandridges, with signs of recent water. The last rains had been patchy, and feed was variable but becoming alarmingly scarce. That day we covered another sixteen miles and crossed seventy-three sandridges. Seventy or more sandridges a day was going to be very hard work for the camels. It meant crossing one every six minutes. We had expected this, but it seemed much worse when theory became actual practice, the endless repetition of the long spinifex-covered approach, the struggle up and through the bank of live sand on the crest, the much steeper stumbling descent to the valley on the far side. I ticked off every ridge as we crossed it with a pencil mark on the compass box before me. We bore to the left as we climbed up, and to the right as we descended, in an attempt to balance the zig-zagging of the course. Sometimes we had to go along the crest for a distance to find a better way down. My latitudes showed that there was a constant slight drift to the south in our easterly course. We were not straightening up enough after coming down the ridges.

Next day the sandridges became even more formidable.

They rose to eighty feet or more, and were all like the big ridge at Andado Station. In the morning we passed through country that had had no rain for at least two years. The spinifex had not flowered for at least a season. There were no seeding stems remaining on it; in fact most of it was quite dead. This was the very height of desolation. There was no fodder at all. At three o'clock in the afternoon we suddenly came into a patch where there had been recent rains, and found ourselves among green spinifex in flower and green canegrass. The whole vista was suddenly green except for the red crests of the sandridges. I thought we had entered the edge of the Queensland rain area, the rains that had brought floods down the Diamantina, and on which the whole expedi¬tion had been planned. In another hour the herbage began to disappear and the aspect become arid again, so we camped. Jack thought I should have camped earlier, but he was being wise after the event. There was a clump of needlebush at this camp, some of it alive, the rest good firewood. There had been rain fairly recently, not long enough ago to affect the herbage, but there were signs that water had run down the sandridges and lain in the low ground.

The rate of progress had been slower to-day. I reckoned we had made twelve miles in six hours; we had crossed fifty-five sandridges, all big ones, and it had been a heavy day.

This was our Camp 8, the eighth halt since we left Andado Bore. We had come ninety-five miles from the bore and were fifty-five miles east of the Hale.

Rain was threatening, so we made a shelter with the large canvas sheet supported by the camel boxes, but only Crocker, Fletcher, Marshall and myself took advantage of it.

The Royal Mail. The unballasted track has sunk into the mud in wet weather. Willochra, 1937.

8

RAIN IN THE DESERT

THE most unexpected thing now happened. We were held up by rain in the middle of the desert! About twenty points fell during the night, enough to make things uncomfortable, and it drizzled gently all next day so that we could not break camp. However, it gave us an opportunity to do some scientific work. Fletcher shot some wrens and chats which were around this camp. Some of them were most brightly coloured and beautiful little birds. Crocker examined the flora and took soil samples and also assisted me to run a three-quarter mile section across the sandridges with level and tape. The nearest sandridge to the camp was found to be sixty-three feet high. Marshall made some film, and Albert had us feeding in undreamt-of luxury.

I finished the preparation of the first of three national broadcasts that were to be given from the desert and expected to put it over that night, but it was postponed on account of poor reception.

Before night we greatly improved the shelter by making a walled enclosure with all the camel saddles and stores, and covering it with the sheet, supporting the centre with a spare piece of pack-saddle wood fixed to the top of the theodolite tripod. This made quite a cosy hut, which attracted Simpson, but still Albert, Jack, Nurie and Andy preferred to stay out under their ground sheets.

The rain increased and fell all night. An inch was measured in a pannikin up to noon next day. Albert slept alongside his fire, and in the morning brought us in the tent a breakfast in bed of bacon on toast with coffee. The rain did not seem to hamper him at all, but it kept the rest of us under cover all day. I read aloud *The Case of the Stuttering Bishop*, which intrigued everybody, and particularly Jack. Mark Twain's story of the golden arm was very successful too. It took Nurie's fancy immensely. At the end he nearly jumped out of what Simpson called our zareba.

We caught about thirty gallons of water on sheets to make. up for what we were using during the delay. Crocker found half a dozen large black water beetles swimming in Simpson's ground sheet. This seemed most mysterious till I found that they had very effective wings and were equally at home in the air. They must have flown in to our camp, but from where? The wind was east, which suggested open water to the east. It was still an intriguing problem.

The wireless transmitter was inside the shelter and that night the first broadcast was attempted. It was very different from giving a talk from a studio, crouched there under the tarpaulin with inadequate light, no table, notes scribbled in pencil and only one hand to hold them, the other being occupied with the little telephone transmitter. The wonder of it appealed strongly to me and I tried to make my listeners feel it too. There were we, in our cramped, cold, damp and ill-lit quarters in the sandridges, hundreds of miles from any signs of human activity, hidden away in the most inaccessible part of Australia's empty wastes, and yet I was talking to people sitting before fires in armchairs a thousand miles away and surrounded by all the luxuries of modern civilization. My voice was in their rooms, a voice from where all else was silence except for the tinkle of the camel bells and an occasional dingo's howl; not even the voice of the cricketer, as Andy called it, is heard in that land. Against the background of our most ancient and primitive way of life and travel the modern scientific equipment showed up in sharp relief, compelling the realization that in civilized places the amenities that science makes available are multiplying so rapidly that appreciation of them is dulled and lags behind. The little wireless plant could bridge three thousand years.

The rain cleared off that night, but the following day was heavily overcast. It was now necessary to dry out before packing up. It is a very bad practice to put wet pack saddles on heavily laden camels, as all the cordage and material has shrunk and hardened and the fit is ruined. We draped all our blankets and equipment over the few needlebushes to air in the wind, which had now changed to south. The day was spent in sketching and studying sand formations. We sank a hole by the camp, between the sandridges, with the post-hole borer, but could only get down eleven feet when sandstone gravel stopped further progress. This was the bottom of the sand and the top of its parent material, the underlying sand-stone. Some of the party trimmed a needle bush and put up signboards on it showing distances to Adelaide and Birdsville. The latter was two hundred miles away as the crow flies, but a good deal further as the camel crosses the sandridge, and Adelaide over seven hundred miles, but the signboard rather incorrectly read, Birdsville 130 and Adelaide 1,004.

There was no more rain. About an inch and a half had fallen, but there was nothing to show for it, no pools of water to be seen lying about. The sand had merely absorbed it as it fell, and was moistened down to a depth of fifteen inches, as we found by digging holes. Where the sand is eleven feet deep even between the sandridges there can be little run-off or accumulation of water on the surface, such as there is with stony ground or ordinary clay soils. Even the desert sands however, are not entirely free of clay, and in heavy rains there may be some run-off from the sandridges, of which in fact we saw some evidence from past rains in little rill-marks down their sides.

Claypans are small low-lying areas with impervious clay bottoms that hold temporary waters. They may be due to the sand having been swept away by local wind eddies, some-times caused by the sandhills themselves, thus exposing a clay floor, or by the run-off from adjacent higher sandy country carrying the finer clay particles down to lower ground and depositing them to make a watertight bottom. They are always very shallow and the water can usually only be relied on for a few weeks, as it is soon lost by evaporation. The claypan is usually from fifty to a hundred yards across. Beyond that they become dry lakes. We were to see many in heavy sandridge country, particularly round Lake Eyre. Some were miles across and were marked as lakes on the map; others were like holes scooped out of the sand, with the sandhills invariably higher around their edges, which strongly suggested that in those cases they owed their origin and continued existence to wind scour.

On the following day, June 17, the fourth day since our arrival, we got away from the wet No.8 Camp to a late start. The wooden sections of the wireless poles had swollen and become jammed in their iron sockets. We heated the joints over the fire till the wood was almost charred, and the whole party engaged in tugs-of-war, all to no effect. It looked as though we would never get them apart. The problem was solved at last by twisting with the pipe grips belonging to the boring set.

The feed around the camp had been poor, but the camels had all day to browse and were still in good condition. They had had no water, but the herbage was damp and the weather cool and moist, so they did not need it. We had made up the four days' water supply the delay had cost us, but Albert's generous catering had made rather serious inroads on the fresh meat. We had been in the desert a week and had only put fifty-five miles behind us in four days of travelling. This rate of progress would have to be increased, but such a hold up would not be likely to occur again, and we reckoned that we should be able to maintain a rate of at least ten miles a day in the worst country we had seen. The feed was not up to expectations - it had only been good through the flooded country along the Hale - but sooner or later we must enter the area affected by the known good season in Queensland. The rains along the telegraph line had not extended into the western side of the desert, but surely we would not have the same ill-luck on both sides! We got away from Camp 8 full of enthusiasm and confidence, refreshed and eager to press on.

Loading up at Charlotte Waters: pack saddles and 16-gallon water canteens.

9
NEAR TO FAILURE

THE new start was most propitious. The camels were rested, the party in high spirits. As we progressed, a clump of trees - probably mulga - was seen to the south between sandridges, and we passed three little pools of surface water. This must have been where the water beetles came from. Two small mobs of budgerigars were noted, and some finches and wrens. A flight of twenty crows seemed interested in us.

The sandridges were big but seemed less formidable to the refreshed cavalcade. Andy, as usual, was running here and there, continually snatching up plants for Crocker or lizards for Fletcher. He had a remarkable memory for what had been already collected, but was rather given to pressing on them what he considered better specimens of the same thing. Towards the end of the day his enthusiasm would often outlast their receptiveness. He was both an example and a task master. It was in the larger field of biology where his contributions were most valuable and most needed. He could always tell at a glance, by its last tracks, whether a reptile or a mouse was in its hole, whether at home or gone visiting, as he said, thus saving a lot of useless digging.

A big lizard of the frill-necked variety was caught that day. Early in the afternoon Andy found the hole of a marsupial rat which he said was at home, so he and Fletcher and others began to dig it out. They thought they would not be long, so elected to stay behind to avoid delay, expecting to catch us up later. I knew the exasperation of trying to overtake a camel string on foot-you gain about half a mile an hour on them, although they seem to be going so slowly. Their long, slow strides are covering a lot more ground than they appear to be. It is when they ate in sight, and then only half a mile away and even within hailing distance, that it becomes so irritating, when you are struggling to close the last short gap and your pride forbids you to call them to halt. It is bad enough on a road, but stumbling 'through the tufts of spinifex was going to make it much worse. However, we meant to camp early, so I left them to gain their experience.

In good country, on tracks, the Australian camel covers about three miles an hour. In hilly country in the MacDonnells I had found two and three-quarter miles an hour a reliable average. In these sandridges I was reckoning on two and a half to two and a quarter, but had so far been unable to check it as there had been no clear nights for longitude observations. The hourly rate of the camel is extraordinarily constant; in fact it is most difficult to vary it. The pack camel cannot be hurried up to any extent, nor does he slow down, but swings along hour after hour at his own fixed gait. This makes route traversing on camels very simple and accurate. It is only necessary to keep a note of the direction and the time of every halt and start. The times are liable to be overlooked at first but it soon becomes a habit to jot them down, like winding on the camera film. At the end of the day the time of marching is added up to the nearest five minutes, and this multiplied by the rate gives the day's run. It is usually possible to check the rate at the beginning of a journey by the time taken between two known points, but we could not check the sandridge rate on our easterly course till I could take a longitude.

We had been told that the first national broadcast had not been a success, and I was to repeat it to-night. The reception had been weak, due probably to the dampness of our equipment. We were also to try a little earlier, soon after sunset, instead of 7.30 p.m. That was the reason for an earlier camp. We had seen nothing of the digging party trailing us up, and had made camp before they appeared. In the valley between sandridges the view ahead or behind was always limited by the next sandridge a few hundred yards away. Even from the crest of a sandridge only two valleys could be seen, each with a. series of crests beyond it, so that to see anyone at a distance it was necessary for both to be on a crest at the same time.

At last the diggers came in, tired and disgruntled, with a quaint story to tell. Before we moved on, a big excavation had been made, Andy working like one possessed. Work apparently went on at the same rate in relays till they had dug themselves out of sight, with shafts and tunnels and regular underground works. The sand was easy to work in, but the amount moved was terrific; and still the hole went on. At last the party began to despair of ever coming to the end of the hole, and questioned Andy more closely on the habits of this subterranean creature. Andy calmly replied, "Him bin dig on fast as you dig after him!" Whether Andy himself ever expected to succeed, perhaps by physical exhaustion of his quarry, or whether he was letting our ignorance overcome his better judgment, was not clear, but the others at once gave up what seemed a hopeless task, picked up their tools and began the weary chase after the camels. When they came into camp even Andy's spirits were damped. It was too bad having the long walk after the failure of the mining operations. Marshall got a good picture of the later stages of the work.

That day I reckoned we had progressed thirteen miles in six hours. We crossed forty-four sandridges, as big as any we had seen. They were rather more irregular and wider on top, without such well-defined crests. The feed had not improved, but was rather worse. There were some green acacia bushes at the camp, of which I had hopes, but Jack said the camels would not eat them. Firewood was very scarce.

It was a miserable camp, with a cold damp wind. Conditions in the open, with poor light, were about as wretched as they could be for a national broadcast, but this time reception had improved, and the broadcast was successfully recorded. Perhaps the conditions were reflected in the reproduction and helped to give it realism and local colour. There was some comfort in the thought.

While we were trying to warm ourselves round the fire something suddenly hit Albert in the back and fell to the ground. It was found to be a bird, attracted by the light of the fire. It had been hard to get specimens of these little birds, but when this one recovered we let it go.

The rain had raised the humidity, and extraordinarily heavy dew became a nightly experience. It was as much trouble as rain. Every night everything became covered with water, the drops all running together to form a veritable layer. We could have used it to augment our water supply, had it not been obvious by this time that water was not going to be our problem, but feed for the camels.

The cheerfulness of the new start scarcely survived the day. The going had been heavy and the feed showed no signs of improving.

Next day we were still in giant sandridges, the biggest yet. They must have reached a hundred feet. They were more symmetrical, with the approach side steeper, and there were sometimes short transverse dunes on the top of them. We made rather a late start owing to the dew, but got in our six hours of travel, and it was quite enough. The going was very heavy, the wider crests with more loose sand greatly increased the camels' tasks. We passed a few little patches of munyeroo during the day, but otherwise it was very barren. In the afternoon some of the camels began to stumble and fall. We pushed on, hoping to find some feed and firewood to camp on, but it became worse. I had to stop. There was some dead needlebush for the fire but no feed at all. Again Jack criticized me for not stopping earlier where there was a little feed, but it was my way to hope for something better ahead and to put the miles behind. The only satisfaction I had that day was to travel hopefully. I reckoned we had made eleven miles, in which we had climbed over forty great masses of sand. They were the highest sandridges we had seen. There was nothing but sand and spinifex between the ridges, no feed, no signs of claypans. A few finches were noticed, a hawk, and a flock of nineteen crows. I wondered if they were the same crows as we had seen the day before, following us. Something sinister about these carrion birds.

It was a quiet and sober camp that night. Things were beginning to look serious. The day's march had definitely given cause for some misgiving. We were not yet half way across the desert, and the camels were beginning to fail. One was developing mange and seemed almost done. There was still over a hundred miles to go to reach the Mulligan, but there could be no question of turning back, for returning was now no easier than go o'er, but on the contrary would be much more difficult if one's expectations about the country ahead proved correct. Jack Bejah was depressed. He spoke of leaving one or two camels behind to follow us if they could, but this would have been against all the principles of exploration. Once you begin to abandon your gear it is a sign of approaching collapse. You should not have any gear you can do without. I told him to redistribute the loads but to keep the string together. It was no good spreading ourselves over the desert. We must come into that Queensland feed any day now.

We were sending a press message almost every night, with a longer one at week-ends, but I had promised Mr. Simpson a special personal one from the middle of the desert. It was hard to decide just where this was. We were now half way to the Queensland border, where we would be in known country, so that this was about the middle of the unknown part and we seemed likely to be near the climax of our difficulties, so I decided to send the message from this camp. It read:

"Mr. A. Simpson, Ru Rua Hospital, North Adelaide. Camp 11, June 18. This is promised message of greetings from the middle of Simpson Desert. All going well. Natural history collections mounting. Beautiful coloured desert wrens and finches, some probably new. Physiographical observations very interesting. No rock so far since leaving River Hale Tablelands. Camels feeling heavy work just now in giant sandridges. Little feed. None to-night but conditions will improve in next few days. All party well. Regards. Best wishes. Madigan". The message was endorsed. "Sent to V.H.U.9., 7.20 p.m; Sunday, June 18, R.A.S".

Mr. Simpson had been in very poor health for some time, and had gone into hospital in a serious condition before we left Adelaide. There was an unhappy possibility that he might not live to hear of the end of the expedition he had financed. Birds were mentioned as he was particularly interested in them.

It was a clear night again at last, and I was able to take star observations. This careful navigation was not really essential, as there had been no features worth fixing since we left the Hale, but there was satisfaction in it. We could go east and strike the Mulligan without even the aid of compasses, but we would not know which side of the old Kaliduwarry Station we were on, and might have difficulty in finding it and waste time in locating ourselves before setting a course for Birdsville. Also I expected to find the course of the Hay River, if nothing else, where no one had seen it before, and this was worth fixing. If disaster should befall us and aeroplanes had to be sent out, we should be able to say exactly where we were; so I took my observations as opportunity offered. This was the first clear night since leaving the Hale, and our first opportunity to fix our position since then. The night was cold, the light poor. Papers, books, maps and instruments were soon wet with dew. Sitting out in the open among the spinifex under these conditions, not to mention considerable physical fatigue, did not help the accuracy of the calculations. I kept making mistakes and finding myself in the Pacific Ocean, which was no place to go to bed in. At last I got it right and was able to pin-point our position on the map. It was 24°44' south and 136°59' east. We had come seventy-eight miles from the Hale in thirty-five and three-quarter hours, giving an average rate of just over two miles an hour. My daily dead reckoning had made it seventy-nine miles, one mile out in seventy-eight. This was the reward for a late night, an aching back and a shivering frame. We might be in considerable difficulty in the worst place in the world, but we knew just where it was. My companions had long ago turned in, quiet and somewhat worried, and were now all fast asleep. I got into my pyjamas as usual, distributed all my clothing along the side of the sleeping bag on the ground sheet, not forgetting boots and socks and hat, else they would be soaking wet in the morning, covered and tucked everything in with the other half of the sheet, and crawled under. I was pleased with the results of my calculations. That feed couldn't be far away now! It was a little bit fuggy shut up in this waterproof and almost air-tight groundsheet, but very warm and comfortable. The camels couldn't stand many more days like to-day, but we could take easier stages. The chronometer was wound and put away in the bottom of Jack's big box-must get a better fastening for that, the piece of stick came out to-day. Nice the way the wireless was working - we must all send more messages home - been neglecting that. We'd be in that feed any day now...

Next morning there was some readjustment of loads, but soon the damp packages were heaved up and the wet cordage knotted, the camels jerked themselves on to their feet, and the long string began to wind slowly over the first sandridge. How were we going to fare today? Across the valley and on to the top of the next sandridge - and there before us lay a small claypan covered with water. Down into the valley, to find the clayey soil was carpeted with munyeroo! No waiting for something better this time. There were a few low mulga bushes at the end of the claypan, a suitable place to camp.

Round to these, and down went the camels, and off came the loads laboriously put on a quarter of an hour before. We would let the camels graze here all day. If we had only come on another half mile last night it would have saved us a lot of work and some anxiety! This water and the green munyeroo must mean the edge of the rain country. Anyway, we would give the camels all the feed they wanted and a spell before tackling the sandridges again. They were soon chewing at great mats of munyeroo pulled up from the ground and dangling from their mouths.

It was a beautiful sunny day. We opened up the baggage and spread everything out to dry, then took a walk round the camp. Two sandridges away to the north-east there was a group of five claypans with gidgee trees, the first gidgee we had seen since leaving the Hale. This certainly looked like the edge of the rain belt. There was more clay here in the soil between the sandridges, and a thinner cover over the underlying rock. Nodules of ironstone lay around, and pieces of chalcedony. Crocker discovered a small rock outcrop of chalcedonized sandstone. More interesting still was the discovery of signs of the former presence of aboriginals, the only such indications seen in the whole desert crossing. These were chips of chalcedony, typical of aboriginal workshop sites where knives, scrapers and spearheads have been made, and also parts of grinding stones, one a piece of schist that must have come from the MacDonnells. This disproved my theory and Winnecke's that aboriginals never entered any part of the desert. It was obvious that in wet seasons they had followed streams down from the ranges to the north, probably only on short visits. We were then not far south of a group of claypans I had mapped during the 1929 aerial reconnaissance. Several claypans had been noted in the northern part of the desert, suggesting that they represented the ends of unnamed streams that come down from the MacDonnells and flood out in the desert. In wet seasons the blacks could obviously follow these streams down from the north, just as Fred Rogers went down the Hay. It was the natives of the east, west and south who had denied all knowledge of the desert, but it was now obviously no more than the southern parts that could be quite unknown to any aboriginal.

The largest of the claypans was only fifty yards across and they held at most a few inches of water. It was too shallow to dip up so some of the party dug a sump in our camp claypan to draw from. When the water in it settled it was still a nice yellow colour, but proved quite good for drinking water. Buckets were filled and put on the fire, and everyone had a hot bath- the first all-over wash for a fortnight. Out of our gallon a day there was enough water for everyone to wash face and hands once a day, but that was

Blacks' camp at Andado The 'wurlies' are made chiefly of bullock hides. Note the big sandridge in the background.

Andado Bore No. 1 The windmill over the bore has been dismantled. Lady boils the billy, and Storm sits on the stones.

was as far as it would go.

The sandridges here were more wavy and broader on top, and the crests of live sand were steep on both sides. There were lower saddles at intervals along the crests giving a jagged profile to the summits. Most of the bigger sandridges showed this saw-tooth effect more or less; the live sand along the crests slopes gently up northwards for a hundred yards or so to a summit and then falls rapidly away to start another rise, thus making serrations along the top of the sandridge. The serrations were more regular and marked in the centre and eastern desert than they were round Andado. Here at this camp they were strongly developed and the saddles between them so pronounced as to make better crossing places. This had not been so for the first sixty miles, when the ridges were practically level along the top and one place was as good as another to cross.

The tension of the last few days was now relieved, and Camp 11 was a very cheerful one. Albert made a pair of beautiful jam tarts. The pastry could not have been bettered. Marshall took some colour films of camp life, in which the tarts showed up to great advantage in a monotonous setting, for the desert colours were practically confined to the red of the sandridges and the grey of the spinifex. There was still very little herbage or green plants, but the munyeroo, now dying off, made brown mats on the lower ground. It is a low, spreading and succulent plant of the portulacca or pig-face family. Again it would have been better to have gone on for another couple of sandridges and camped among the rather poor and scattered gidgee at the next claypans, but this camp was quite good enough. I had ridden on to the crest of the next sandridge before deciding to off-load, but still another sandridge denied us the view of the group of claypans and trees that lay beyond.

Andy was in great form this night. He loved a good camp. Now everything was rosy for him. He said, "This life good, walkabout, homestead no good, live longer this way", a very profound truth as applied to him and all his people. I don't think he had ever seen the sea, but when something lead the conversation to it he said he didn't like the sea-"too wet, no tracks, land more better." I was sitting aside writing notes while the rest of the party talked, and I took the opportunity of recording some of Andy's remarks, which were a constant entertainment to us. His conversation was always jerky consisting of short statements without elaboration and often with little connection, like a series of wise-cracks. It was often interesting to try and fill in the gaps that he left blank in his train of thought. Andy went on: "Can't sleep during day. Night long enough. Last night too long, make my jaw ache. First one side then the other. This fellow clever more top (God). Bring down water, ducks, plenty. (Ly-Ly did not know of God. He expressed his pleasure at a good camp more crudely, with his bloody widgetty, bloody yam, bloody mobs.) At Marree they think I not come-too many people-country too dry. At Warrina my people say not go-Frank say not go. I say I chance myself - never mind perish". Andy was boasting now. For the past two days he had obviously been wishing he had not come. It was interesting to hear that his people had warned him not to come, at Marree and again at Warrina. It was Jack who had turned the scale. At Andado he was still undecided.

As I had missed the time signals for a couple of nights I made sure of getting them that night, and as it was clear I took further observations to check our position. The results agreed sufficiently well. We were about seven miles south-west of the claypans I had mapped from the air, so I decided to go north-east next day to locate them. Those we were at seemed too small to be the same. I also wanted to check the position of the claypans, which had been plotted only from dead reckoning in the middle of a five-hour flight.

We left Camp 11 next day, June 20, and started on the north-east course. We were now travelling obliquely to the sandridges and thus crossing fewer. They were becoming smaller, too, so that the going was much easier. We passed the first group of claypans, and then another pair of small ones beyond the next sandridge, one surrounded by munyeroo, the other in quite a grove of gidgee. After a few more sandridges we came to the south end of a broad valley of gidgee, with trees visible to the horizon. A sandridge came to an end here, and we rounded its northern extremity. This was the only end of a sandridge we saw in the whole desert journey, the only one we did not have to cross. There was probably a claypan up in the gidgee. We did not investigate, but continued on our course and were soon crossing sandridges again.

Later in the morning I saw a big brown snake that disappeared down a hole. We halted to dig it out. The hole was a long one, probably a mouse hole, and followed a log buried in the sand. Andy as usual dug with the excitement of a terrier. At last we came to the snake at the end of the hole and pinned it with a forked stick and eventually killed it. It was a venomous species nearly six feet long.

The country was improving and green herbage began to appear. We crossed another valley, or inter-ridge space, with gidgee trees in it, then one with a stony patch in the middle, and in the next we came on a wide claypan a couple of hundred yards across covered with about two inches of water. We tried the camels at it but only a few of them wanted to drink. After another wooded valley, at the end of seven miles on the north-east course, we turned east again. In the next two miles we passed four claypans, the last surrounded on all sides by sandhills, a regular hole in the sand like those we were to see later near Lake Eyre. This one was about three hundred yards by a hundred and fifty, and had about an inch of water on it. We went on for another couple of miles without seeing any more claypans, and camped. This was obviously the group of claypans I had seen from the air, and gratifyingly close to where I had placed them; in fact as accurately placed as such an area could be, without plotting each individual claypan.

The sandridges were now only about thirty feet high, and closer together. There was green sandhill wattle about, and green spinifex and canegrass, with plenty of camel feed. There had been several halts on this day. We had covered about twelve miles and crossed thirty-nine sandridges. It had been a very interesting day, with more variety than we had known so far in the desert. At every mile the vegetation was improving and there was already abundance of feed. The day's march had put it beyond doubt that we had entered the Queensland rain belt and there was nothing further to worry about. It was only a matter of time and the other side of the desert would be reached. For a few days we had been haunted by the possibility of failure, but those days were behind and the crisis was passed. The rest should be easy ... It was more obvious than ever that the journey would be impossible except after exceptionally good seasons, and even then the desert would present some difficult patches. The distance is short, but the going so heavy that progress must be slow, and good feed for camels is thus essential. The journey cannot be hurried by day-and-night travel, as the camels must be given frequent rests, and six hours' march a day is enough in the heavier parts. That night we knew that success was sure. A message was sent to the University of Adelaide.

At the cairn on Poodnitera Hill Left to right: Ly-Ly, Nurie, Fletcher, Madigan, Crocker, Hubbard.

Allua Soak, Hale River Filling up the canteens.

10

DANGER PAST, WE REACH THE HAY

THE journey now became more carefree, and a spirit of light-heartedness manifested itself in various ways, one of which was an outburst of enthusiasm for knife-throwing. A sheath knife worn on the belt sailor-fashion, a thin butcher's knife, not a Boy Scout's dagger, is one of the most useful things you can have on any sort of expedition, and every member of the party carried one. I had made rather an impression at Andado by throwing mine into posts, and now the party settled down to steady practice, so that it was not long before I had to look to my laurels. Several of them continually threw their knives ahead as they walked along. It was Simpson's ambition to transfix a lizard, but I do not think he ever achieved it.

Competitions were staged in camp, with the whole party standing in a ring round a target on the ground.

We decided to have a short halt at noon in the future to eat some lunch. Albert cooked some very fruity cakes for the purpose, and filled water bottles with tea after breakfast each morning. The lunch was put in one of Jack's boxes that had a lower compartment. with side door and could be opened from the ground, so that it was easily got at and the camels remained standing while we had our quarter-hour snack. Those hunks of raisin conglomerate became something to look forward to.

One day Andy found some feathers, and then the buried remains of a wild turkey. He carefully re-buried it. He said, "Dog save 'em up for puppy - sluts all big now - soon have puppies". He had found half a rabbit buried in the sand away back at the Hale and buried it again. He would not rob the dingo and her puppies. Dingo tracks were now to be seen along the crests of every sandridge.

Most of us took turns at walking and riding to vary the monotony. Andy, Crocker and Fletcher spent most of their time walking and collecting. The rain had cleared away by now and it was warm and sunny all day, though still cold and wet from the dew at night and in the early morning. The routine was by this time well established. Jack always woke before daylight, at about 6.30 a.m. I would wake to find Albert, Jack, Nurie and Andy already standing round a fire, their swags rolled up, the camels out of the yard and feeding, and some tea ready, for it is the bushman's invariable custom to have some tea and stand round the fire for a while at dawn before he begins the work of the day. Everyone rolled up his swag, often wet, as soon as he got out of it, and then after the customary stand round the fire, breakfast was eaten, the camels were brought in, and loading started. While the loading was being done by the four, there was a chance for the scientific staff to do a little collecting and note making. At every camp I took the direction of the sandridges, which never varied more than two degrees from 3320 true bearing from side to side of the desert, and at intervals also measured their height. Fletcher brought in his rat traps, which were always empty. Crocker had a look at the plants, and Marshall and Simpson dismantled and packed up the wireless. It only took a few minutes for each to load his own camel, thanks to the convenience of the police pack-bags, but the pack camels were a considerably longer job. Before their loads were ready the breakfast things had to be washed up and stowed away, and there was still some equipment that was too long to go in the boxes or bags, like theodolite legs and shovels and boring gear, and these had to be made up into bundles and tied on. The bundles were never undone if it could be avoided, as with the staff officer who hesitated to consult his map because of the problem of folding it up again. In spite of all our attempts to hasten camp-breaking it was more often after nine o'clock than before by the time we finally got on the move. Then followed about six hours of steady travelling with only one stop of a quarter of an hour for lunch. This time of march was later increased to seven or eight hours when conditions became easier.

Albert and his little camel usually provided some comic relief to the monotony of the day's march. He was just a passenger, and never made any attempt to control the camel, usually riding with his hands in his pockets. The camel went where it liked, sometimes with its nose at my elbow and taking an occasional bite at my sleeve, sometimes lagging behind to feed, after which it would give a few bucks and then run to catch up, causing Albert much alarm, but never any damage. It was not above sitting down if it felt tired. Some of the riders used to encourage it to lag behind the string with them and then they would trot forward again and leave it. This ruse always made it play up, to everyone's amusement but Albert's.

At the evening camp Albert would have hot tea ready twenty minutes after the camels went down. He would snatch the makings out of one of the big tucker boxes as soon as it hit the ground and have the tea made before the rest of the unloading was finished and the camels hobbled.

We each had our own ideas about the best place to unroll our swags in for the night. Jack liked what he called clean ground, which meant the barest, highest and hardest he could find. He scorned to put any brushwood under his sheet at any time. The crown of a concrete road would have been his ideal. Nurie followed suit. Andy was always away by himself, usually with a little fire of his own and mostly with a bed of bushes, sometimes over him as well as under. Albert slept close alongside his fire amongst his equipment, and Marshall was attracted by the supposed warmth of the fire. Simpson was prone to shovel up a mound of sand, especially if it was wet, and sleep in a basin at the top of it. Crocker, Fletcher and I scattered ourselves round the outskirts. I preferred clean sand to Jack's hard places, and always sought some brushwood if the weather was wet.

It was usually dark before dinner was ready, but we had the two petrol-vapour lamps, which were Marshall's special care. While the meal was being prepared and served, and the yard made and the camels finally brought in, the scientists had time to label their specimens and write up their notes, while Simpson unpacked the wireless gear, put up the aerials and prepared for the nightly contact with Harry Ding.

Before leaving the Hale I had appointed Fletcher as second in command, which did not involve any duties unless I should become a casualty. Besides his photography, Marshall assisted Simpson with the wireless and Albert with the cooking. When the pedal generator was used Marshall got plenty of leg exercise, but fortunately for him we found the batteries were really better. I took the chronometer comparison with the time signal at seven o'clock, and sometimes had star observations to make in the evening. We were usually all under the blankets by nine o'clock, by which time it was generally very cold and we were glad to get under cover, for in the desert there was never enough wood for a decent warming fire.

Out in the open it is a fallacy to think that there is any advantage in sleeping beside a fire. You must have unlimited firewood, and get up every hour or two to make up the fire, and also you must sleep so close to it, if you are to get any benefit at all, that you get holes burnt in your blankets from sparks, which happened to several of our party. The wild blackfellow sleeps between two fires in the winter and frequently gets very severely burnt by putting arms and legs into the fire, but he, of course, has no covering, and must rely on fire for any extra warmth at night.

June 21 was the date for the next national broadcast at Camp 13. We camped early that day, after covering thirteen miles and crossing seventy-four small sandridges. The big sandridges were always more evenly spaced and further apart, the smaller ones closer and more irregular. It seemed as if groups of smaller ones might eventually form one large one. I had announced at the first broadcast that next time Andy would be on the air, a full-blooded aboriginal speaking to Australia, which would be something new to broadcasting, and coming from the heart of the desert would make it even more unique. It was arranged that Andy should say a few words, and then sing a corroboree song. We had some rehearsals of this, and on the night before Andy had given a splendid performance. He lost all his diffidence and put his whole heart into it, leaping and gesticulating as he warmed up to his theme. He was soon quite unconscious of his surroundings, and became transfigured. We watched him lose contact with us and drift into another world, a mysterious spirit world, where he was a stranger to us. It was eerie in the desert darkness. We could not hope to put the full effects of this performance on the air. Andy would have to sit down and hold the telephone transmitter and could never get into the spirit of it without the action. He said the song was about a "dorg", or dingoes, but it was not clear why it led up to such dramatic intensity of feeling. Later we gave him a rehearsal with. the telephone, under the pretence that it was going on the air, but I do not think he was deceived, as he seemed so little disconcerted; there was too much levity going on at the time.

When the time arrived for the actual transmission we had the transmitter on a small sandridge near the camp. I gave my talk and then introduced Andy. I could see his confidence oozing away as the moment approached. He was to say a few words about the song by way of introduction, but by the time I handed him the 'phone he was speechless. It was a lot to expect of him, and for a moment I thought all was lost. At last he found a still, small voice and said "Dog all about. Singum good song", and went straight into the song. It lacked the fire of previous performances, but it did not falter, and the sequence of strange cadences sounded quite typical, and I believe went over very well. He gained more confidence towards the end, and when finished, called quite boldly, "Good luck all people in Australia!" It was a good impromptu end, and showed he realized what he was doing. Later in the evening he suddenly said, "My nerves all gone".

When Andy had finished, Jack, son of the grand old man Bejah Dervish was introduced, and Jack said a few modest words that could not convey a picture of the fine sturdy fellow that he was, a key man of the expedition.

I observed for latitude that night, as the course had been rather irregular and I was not sure how much northing we had made.

Camp 13 was little more than twenty miles from my aerially determined position for the Hay River, so we should reach the river in a day and a half. The sandridges were now more like sandbanks, with rounded and irregular crests and small hollows and mounds on them. They were only from ten to thirty feet high and were not conspicuous. Between Camp 13 and Camp 14 we crossed eighty in sixteen miles without difficulty. A few days before we had seemed shut in by a close sky-line jagged with high and menacing sandridge crests, in a red, forbidding and hostile landscape, but now the low smooth ridges no longer obscured the distant horizon, and the stems of the seeding spinifex gave to the whole wide view the friendly appearance of a vast yellow cornfield.

For most of the journey there was deep sand in the lanes between the ridges, with nothing growing there but spinifex. In a few places where the sand was thinner there was scattered needle bush, and round the claypans, where there was no loose sand, gidgee was always found, otherwise there was nothing but spinifex in the lanes. All the other vegetation, shrubs and annuals, was concentrated on the sandridges themselves, and specially along the crests in the live sand. This always seemed a paradox. Surely there must be more moisture in the lower ground and better water-holding properties, yet all the greenery was on the ridges! Perhaps the seed is swept away from the valleys and buried and preserved better on the ridges. One theory put forward is that the water is more available in the porous sand of the ridges than in the more clayey lanes, and the plant roots can there drain it to the last drop. This difference in porosity between the live sand of the ridges and the denser soil of the lanes is probably the real reason for the better growth of plants on the ridges. The rainfall readily soaks into the sand and may sink beyond the range of capillarity and thus escape loss by evaporation to a large extent, forming a damp layer available to roots below a dry surface. With less penetration and greater capillarity all the soil moisture is soon lost by evaporation.

Now there was flowering wattle and grevillea, canegrass, hop-bush, buckbush, water bush and many other herbs and grasses on the ridges, becoming more luxuriant every day. Parrot flower with its curious green blooms like miniature birds, typical of the south-west of Queensland, was seen here for the first time, and several wild turkeys were noted, the first since we had left the Finke.

I thought that it had been made clear before we left that telegrams for us would be accepted by the P.M.G.'s Department, addressed to the expedition via Yunta, to be transmitted to us over the air by Harry Ding, but we had had very few personal messages, so we requested the Broadcasting Commission to announce it again. On the next night at Camp 14 everyone got a message from home except Andy. It was later noticed that Andy had gone very silent and sad, and it occurred to Simpson to get a message for him as well, so this was staged. I called to Simpson to listen in again in case any further messages were to hand, and Simpson went to the receiver and after a while had an imaginary conversation with Harry Ding, with all the usual conventions of the Inland wireless, which included a stereotyped intonation, repetition of each phrase, and much "Over to you, Harry, over to you", of which Simpson was now a master. Soon he had a message of greetings and good wishes from Col. Thomas written out on a slip of paper, and gave it to Andy. Andy could not read it, but put it in the pocket of his shirt, and was once more his enthusiastic self. Like British Israelites, he had a way of foretelling events after they had happened, or bringing up all sorts of mystic evidence which should have foretold them. He said, "all day he feel people thinking about him down there". It made him very happy. It seemed a pity that it was a deception.

On June 23 we got away from Camp 14 at 8.50 a.m. for the last run to the Hay River. At 11 a.m. we passed a few box gums, where there were galahs and budgerigars, and at 11.15 a.m. came upon a wide valley several hundred yards across, well covered with trees and bushes. I rode on for another mile to make sure it was not merely a branch of the main stream but there was nothing but sandridges beyond. This dry and sandy valley was the Hay River. We went downstream for a mile and camped among gum trees and flowering wattle, the best camp of the whole journey, with the possible exception of the first Hale River camp.

The last of the national broadcasts was to be given this night, and it was a very suitable occasion, for now the unknown was behind us. Winnecke in 1883 had come down the Hay to a point about five miles upstream from this camp, and the Queensland border, surveyed in 1882, was only twenty-three miles away. The Mulligan River, where there had been cattle stations, was another forty miles to the east of the border. We were practically on known ground, and about a hundred and fifty miles from human habitations at Birdsville. Feed was plentiful, the water in hand was more than we would need, the desert was conquered! We were not yet quite out of the wood, but we could whistle with confidence. It was only a matter of walking in to Birdsville about ten days away. We had taken just a fortnight to cross from the Hale to the Hay, through a hundred and twenty-five miles of untraversed desert and across five hundred sandridges.

We decided to make a good camp, and to celebrate the occasion. Crocker had the luck to shoot a turkey and Albert started to prepare a feast. A turkey was just what was wanted. The poor bird could not have shown up at a more opportune moment. We made the first good fire since leaving the Hale, this time with gum logs, not the twisty needlewood sticks of the desert, and the smell of the burning leaves was incense. I did myself well with a thick spring mattress of blossoming wattle boughs, and several others made themselves soft and fragrant couches.

For the last broadcast each member was to have a minute of the programme, except Jack and Andy, who had already spoken. These minute speeches had been written out and rehearsed and pruned for several days before, and brought to each speaker's satisfaction. No record of the speeches was kept but the speakers were introduced as Crocker, botanist - an old companion and a most industrious collector; Fletcher, biological collector and genial humourist of the party; Hubbard, cook and one of the best men in camp one could find; Marshall, photographer, young in the ways of the bush but learning in a good school; Nur Mahommet Moocha-Nurie for short-Bejah's assistant, with the nimblest of fingers on a camel's nosepeg; and Simpson, who had made a great success of the wireless, and could turn out no mean damper. The broadcast ended with a personal message to Mr. Simpson in hospital, telling him that the successful crossing of his desert was now assured.

When the broadcast was finished, Albert put on his dinner of stuffed roast turkey. It was a really excellent meal. The nine of us ate our fill, and still a meal remained. To everyone's astonishment, Marshall produced a bottle of whisky, which gave a final touch to the festive board. It was apparently the need of some Dutch courage for the broadcast that had brought this treasure to light, but it could not have chosen a better occasion for emerging from its hiding place.

I observed for position that night and fixed Camp 15 on the Hay River. It was a cold night, with the first frost since the rains.

We were all looking forward to another meal of cold turkey.

Albert left it on a box near his head and when he woke in the morning he found it had disappeared without leaving a trace. Even Andy had no explanation for this. It must have been a cat or a dingo that took it but Andy could find no tracks. The ground was rather leafy round about but still he was inclined to take a supernatural view. It just vanished and that was the end of it. We wished we could have eaten more the night before.

Next day we went down the valley of the Hay for ten miles and again camped in its bed. The river here at its lower end can be described as a broad sandy valley full of trees and shrubs, running parallel to the sandridges, with a waste of sandridges and spinifex each side of it. The valley varies in width from two hundred to four hundred yards, occasionally opening up into box-gum flats and then narrowing down, but keeping a very straight course of about south-east by south. Only one small channel was seen in the valley, with occasional wider swamp areas. There were no signs of large volumes of running water ever passing down, no drift wood or scour, and no gravel, only fine red sand everywhere. It was like a dead river valley. At one point there was a patch of about a hundred yards of stone along the channel floor, a flinty crust, showing that rock was not far below. Stunted box gums were everywhere in the valley, with acacias and various shrubs. Birds were fairly plentiful, though where they got their water was a mystery. Possibly the dew was sufficient for them at that time. We saw no water in the ten miles we traversed the valley, and knew of none within fifty miles. There were large flocks of budgerigars, several galahs, and crows, hawks, zebra finches nesting, and some other small birds. We saw only one turkey, the one that Crocker shot.

I observed again that night for position as a check, arid found we were seventeen miles west of the Queensland border at a point eighty-six miles north of Poeppel's corner. The longitude gave the position of the river about where Winnecke had placed it, and agreed with my aerial observations, and with a longitude taken on a former expedition near the Tarlton Range, 150 miles upstream at the head of the Hay. The course of the river is practically a straight line parallel to the sandridges. Existing maps show the Hay about ten miles too far to the east.

I blazed a gumtree in the river at this camp, Camp 16, on the largest tree we could find, which was only about a foot in diameter. After removing the bark half way round I cut into the wood with a chisel in the conventional way. I would be much interested to know who next sees this tree.

Simpson had dropped his knife somewhere in the ten miles we had travelled in the Hay valley, and Andy went back to find it. He came back with it all right, but said he thought he was never going to find it and was wondering what to do, when he thought of turning his hat round the other way. As soon as he did this, there was the knife on the ground in front of him.

I had seen the rabbit-proof fence marking the Queensland border at Tobermorey Station, and had it in my mind that this fence ran right down to Poeppel's corner, although I knew that the corner of the State of Queensland had been cut off by a fence running up on the west side of the Mulligan. I expected to come to a fence at the border next day and even hoped to find the eighty-sixth mile post on it, for I knew Wells had put small pegs in at every quarter mile and good posts with the mileage carved on them at every mile.

Setting a course in the desert. Madigan takes bearings from the crest of a sandridge.

11

THE MULLIGAN AT LAST

NEXT morning we set off due east to find the border fence, seventeen miles away. Two or three little claypans were passed on the east side of the river bed, all dry. There were some clumps of bushy mulga and some old hakeas, but the country was much drier again, with little feed. The sandridges were higher, up to fifty feet, and the spinifex very dense and dry, with the sand blown away from the bushes and the camels having to pick their way between the tufts. This patch had missed the rains and we were back in desert conditions again, actually in the country where Sturt turned back in 1845, and his description, quoted before, exactly fitted it.

Later in the morning I saw a large snake and got off my camel and started beating it with my camel whip, which was not very effective and only slightly stunned it. Andy came running up from the rear and shouted to me to desist and at once picked up the snake and began to treat it with sympathy, even affection. It was a womma, a harmless carpet snake. Everyone had to handle it then, and most of the party were photographed with it round their necks.

Everyone was looking forward to seeing the fence, the first sign of civilization. We should arrive at it about five o'clock. That time came, and passed, and there was nothing to be seen. We went on till sunset, about half past five, and still no indication of a border line, no fence, no mile posts. We came to a little dry claypan lined with gidgee, and camped. We had come a good seventeen miles and I felt confident that we had crossed the border, but it was disappointing to see nothing. I fancied my companions were a little doubtful of my navigation as they well might be, whereas I had hoped to impress them by finding the eighty-sixth mile post. I was reminded afterwards in Birdsville that this portion of the border had never been fenced, a thing I should have remembered. The old rabbit-proof fence south of Birds ville runs along the Queensland-South Australian border to a point ten miles west of the Mulligan and forty-five miles east of the Northern Territory border at Poeppel's Corner, and from there it runs north along the west side of the Mulligan, finally coming in to the Northern Territory border at a point over two hundred miles north of Poeppel's Corner, and just south of the Toko Ranges, "thus cutting off the south-west corner of Queensland. The fence is no longer maintained, and west of Birdsville it is completely buried in sand in places. At one time they used to rebuild it over the top of the buried parts, but now the rabbits could walk over if they wanted to, though there is not much to be gained by it. There was no fence where we crossed into Queensland, and it would have been a bit of exceptional luck if we had seen a" mile post. The pegs are probably buried or eaten by white ants, but the posts should be standing although they were put in over sixty years ago. Colson found the corner post still standing at Poeppel's Corner, with the lettering clear to read. We camped on the border on June 26, at Camp 17.

I now decided to take a straight course for a bend in the Mulligan rabbit-fence near old Kaliduwarry Station. This was thirty-nine miles away on a true bearing of 1360, according to my reckoning, that is, south-east, so we had finished with crossing the sandridges almost at right angles and would now take them more obliquely, which would mean fewer to cross in a day's march. On the last day we had crossed sixty-seven, the one nearest to the border camp being thirty-eight feet high. There was no need now to bother about the doubtful Mudloo Well as we had plenty of water to see us through. This course would take us a little to the south of its marked position.

It was three days' march to Kuddaree waterhole at Kaliduwarry Station. The first day showed a marked change in the country. Instead of dense spinifex between the sandridges there were clumps of gidgee, gradually becoming more continuous till they ran for miles along the valleys. This means better rainfall and more clayey soil. The country became greener again, with annuals on the crests of the sandridges, parrot flower, flannel flower and grasses. The sandridges had been more straggly on each side of the Hay, but now they were straight again, higher and with more defined crests and live sand on top, favouring the annual plants, and with flatter valleys between. We crossed only sixteen ridges that day, on the oblique course, in fifteen miles, and fifteen on the following day in the same distance.

Marshall filmed the arrival at Camp 18, showing the making of camp; Jack's dog getting down from his tuckerbox, the rapid unloading, and Albert's speed with the tea, were the high lights.

Camp 19 was the last desert camp, for we would reach the Mulligan next day. The adventure was nearly over and the task done; the glamour was fading. Indeed, it is better to travel hopefully than to arrive. The rest would be easy. I suffered a reaction from the strenuous days, and was tired. Perhaps this was the last of the hard journeys I had started out upon so hopefully twenty-eight years before, to end them in this desert place. For some of the young men in the party it was the first real living they had known, but they had all before them. Would I ever be out on the trail again?

We had seen no traces of the Leichhardt expedition though we had kept the possibility in mind right through. This did not prove anything, as even if that expedition had perished in the desert, which I believe to be the case, the chances of finding any trace of them in a single crossing would be very remote. There is a story, largely discounted, of blacks reporting their presence on the Mulligan River to an early traveller.

This camp was in a grove of gidgee that stretched as far as the eye could see up and down the inter-sandridge flat. Vegetation was plentiful in the live sand along the crests of the ridges, and on the flats there was small buck-bush and quite a lot of saltbush. Spinifex was thinning out.

We were away next morning at nine o'clock to find the angle in the rabbit fence, from which another fence ran east for five miles to the river and the old station. Later in the morning we crossed a big dry lagoon extending as far as we could see to the north and south. It was about three miles west of the rabbit fence and was not marked on the Queens-and maps. Its surface was a glaring white, like the pipeclay track on the Coorong in South Australia. After lunch I saw a large copper-coloured snake which disappeared in bushes and we were unable to find it. The sandridges became low and rounded, giving the country a gently rolling appearance, and at half-past two we suddenly arrived at the fence. It was only a derelict-looking affair, a boundary that had not been "ridden" for years, yet it was the handiwork of man, and at its sight the whole dreary aspect of the place was changed to one of friendliness, the desert atmosphere was dissipated in the twinkling of an eye. We photographed the party string¬ing along beside it. I picked up a rusty tobacco tin and a small ointment pot gone purple from the action of the sun's rays. They seemed objects of the greatest interest.

Now, from this westerly projecting angle in the fence, one part ran east of north and the other east of south, the southern part being set back a mile along the east-west fence, with a catch paddock between them. If we missed the corner on its south side we would not meet the fence till considerably south of the corner, which is exactly what happened. I wanted to come right in on the sharp corner of this paddock at the end of two hundred miles of desert navigation, but we met the fence in a straight, and I went on down it for nearly a mile before it occurred to me that I might be south of the corner. A compass bearing along the fence showed this to be the case, and we turned back. On the way back we came to a claypan covered with water, and made a halt. Some of the camels had a drink, their first for eight days, but they did not drink much and others would not touch the water at all. It was a mile and three-quarters from where we first met the fence back to the east-west fence that runs from the corner to the river. As we came back we saw no paddock fence at all. It had probably been. removed, being a private fence, when the station was closed, if indeed it had ever been on the ground as well as on the map, so there was no paddock corner. When I plotted our course back from the point of first meeting the fence it passed right over the paddock corner on the map. This was very satisfactory, to have passed over the point, but not nearly as thrilling as it would have been to see it appear before us. And we had wasted an hour and a half in locating ourselves.

We halted to boil up some tea at the inner corner, and then started on the last five miles to the Mulligan River along the fence. There were some wire netting rabbit traps along the fences near the corner, but we saw no rabbits about.

It was after sunset when we started on the last two hours' ride, but dusk soon gave way to bright moonlight. The country was bare and undulating, with broad rounded sandridges and little live sand. We crossed several claypans, glaring white in the moonlight. This last two hours seemed very long. The moonlight gave a rigidity and unreality to the scene, and seemed to intensify the silence. The country became flatter, with dry swamps in which· stood scattered and dead box gums stretching upwards their bleached and ghostly limbs. Complete silence fell on the party, where a last joyous scramble might have been expected. Nineteen camels and nine men were stealing along through the moonlight without a sound. In the lead I could not hear even the soft padding of the broad feet in the sand, but only the occasional creak of a pack saddle.

Then cloud came over and the moon was obscured. It was difficult to see any distance. I began to wonder if the great white claypans might not be the Mulligan River. We had no idea what the river was like. Perhaps it was only a string of claypans with occasional waterholes. We passed a gate in the fence, and a quarter of a mile beyond came to another flat with dead box gums. We had made the distance, so I camped on the side of a broad sandridge on the edge of this dry swamp. Crocker and I went back to the gate and through it, thinking the old homestead might be there, but after making a wide circuit we came back to camp without finding anything. Simpson and Fletcher went along the fence, and came back saying they had found a better-defined channel with a waterhole, and a hut on a sandhill beyond it about a mile away. This seemed likely to be the station, so we prepared for the night, satisfied that the camp was on the Mulligan and the desert was crossed.

In the moonlight it was very difficult to tell whether there was water in the claypans or not. They all had white surfaces. We had passed a small one near the gate and a discussion arose as to whether it had water in it. I thought it was water. Jack thought it was mud. We had the usual bet on it, a bottle of beer at Birdsville - by this time balances were being struck as to each member's liability over these bets - and some of us went back to investigate. The claypan was found to be covered with white colloidal mud, with practically no water. That there was not a cupful of water had been the bet, and I think I won, but not very satisfactorily, as I expected to find much more than that. The claypan was only twenty feet or so across and we had passed very close to it. In the middle, in the dampest spot, we found a small lone frog and brought it back for the spirit bottle.

Rain was now threatening so we erected the tarpaulin again.

I did not get under it. It rained during the night, but I slept through it and woke rather wet, as the water had got between the folds of my ground sheet. Andy had camped on the top of the sandhill. He told us next day he was frightened there would be a flood, on account of the frog, which was sitting up in the mud praying for more rain to come. He did not like the frog being put into the spirits. He had been rather worried about the collecting all along, his keenness to please and show his knowledge conflicting with his sympathy for the victim. He was always expecting it to bring us bad luck. He sometimes wanted to let lizards go, and one Sunday he did release one. He was very particular about Sundays. He said swearing was bad on Sunday morning, not so bad in the afternoon, more better not swear at all. The Christian teaching he had received as a child at the Kilalpaninna Mission had left an indelible impression, but was somewhat mixed with his own tribal beliefs and superstitions, in fact was superimposed on them without destroying them, for their roots were very deep. What the mother teaches is never entirely lost. He considered that Simpson, Crocker and Fletcher all swore too much, and particularly Fletcher, to whom something might happen -"You might fall off camel or camel might fall over on a sandhill". This was the only prophesy of Andy's that ever came true, for on the very day that he made the remark Fletcher's camel did roll him off on to some spinifex. The same day a mountain devil lizard was found and Andy said, "Devil him sometimes very bloody clever. Too much swearing and only catchem devil lizard".

There seemed to be something in Andy's foreboding on this occasion for it rained lightly all day and everything was miserably wet again.

We still had seventy-seven gallons of water in our canteens left from the two hundred and thirty-two we had started out with, plus the thirty we had caught on tarpaulins, so the nine men had used one hundred and eighty-five gallons in nineteen days-an average of nearly ten gallons a day, or one gallon a man. We had relaxed the water restrictions towards the end, but not much more had been used.

Thirty-one sandridges had been crossed on the last day, making a grand total of seven hundred and six from Andado Station to the Mulligan.

It would now be impossible to move till the rain stopped.

We found that we were on a branch of the Mulligan, a series of swamps with a better-defined channel a mile away. The hut on the high sandridge was beside the fence and was a deserted boundary rider's hut. The river took a turn round the end of the sandridge. The Kuddaree waterhole was at the north end of the sandridge, a wonderful sheet of water six hundred yards long, a hundred yards wide and several feet deep, with black swans on it, teal and several other species of duck, and cranes. There were large flocks of white cockatoos (corellas) in the green trees, and some galahs. At a smaller waterhole further east and a mile and half from the camp, we found the remains of the old Kaliduwarry Station. It was built of boughs and thatch and most of the roof had fallen in. It was a desolate looking place, surrounded by mud. I shot a few ducks on the water and Marshall got some more. The water was wide and the cover small, so they were difficult to get. Before the day was over water was lying about in all the swamps.

That night we sent messages to the press, to Mr. Simpson and to our families, telling them that we had reached the Mulligan and the desert crossing was finished. We were then seventy-five miles from Birdsville or about four days' journey.

The next day was fine and we spread everything out to dry. Everyone bathed and shaved, and we took the opportunity to make some repairs to clothing and equipment.

When we first started out the Birdsville wireless was out of action, as the operator, Bob Gaffney, was away at Marree and could not return on account of the state of the track. Now he was back again and we were in touch with Birdsville, where we were told a welcome was awaiting us.

On the first of July we left Camp 20 on the Mulligan and began the last stage of the journey into Birdsville. We intended to follow the Mulligan down to Annandale Station, a day's journey of nineteen miles, from where we expected to find a track leading to Birdsville.

We started off along the branch of the river we were camped on, which was by now a series of shallow lakes. The going was wet and slippery, of the sort that the camel abhors. After a mile we managed to cross the low ground to the sandridge which separated the two branches of the river, and continued on down the left bank of the branch on the edge of the sand. In the afternoon we crossed the dividing sandridge, as it was becoming lower, and entered the valley of the' main stream, which was there very well defined, a channel about six feet deep and twenty-five yards across. There was a high sandridge on its far side as well. Like the Hay, the Mulligan runs *between* the sandridges and parallel to them. We followed along the edge of this sandridge, which ended - or began - at an open space or backwater, and in this we found the track from Kaliduwarry to Annandale, faint and hard to follow. It began to rain again, and the rain steadily increased. After a hour of it I decided to camp, although then only a couple of miles from Annandale. If that place proved to be anything like Kaliduwarry there was nothing to be gained by going on there, in the way of shelter. So we made camp on the side of the sandridge on the left bank of the river. We made a good camp with the tarpaulin and even put up a ground sheet for Albert to cook under.

There were scrubby gum trees all about, with many hollows in them, and in almost every hollow there was a budgerigar's nest. We could hear the young birds squawking for food whenever we approached an occupied hollow trunk or limb. It rained steadily, but Albert put on a splendid dinner of braised duck.

After four weeks of sandridges in the desert, this first day of level going down the Mulligan had been a wonderful change and relief. We had crossed only one sandridge all day. There was no bother about keeping on a course. The track had been a welcome sight. It seemed just too easy to be following a road, and gave one an extraordinarily comfortable and carefree feeling.

The river bed was lined with better-grown box gums, and the valley floor was covered with good feed, salt bush, buck-bush, marsh-mallows and grasses. There was some "dead-finish" about too, a straggly and thorny acacia of the most derelict and melancholy appearance, whose name most aptly fits it. It's only use is for firewood, and that only in the direst extremity, although I am told it makes a good stockwhip handle. There had been no saltbush in the desert, even along the Hay, till well after the Queensland border was passed, but at Camp 19, halfway from the border to the Mulligan, there was quite a lot between the sandridges on the gidgee flats, with small buckbush as well. Limey nodules had been noticed on those flats.

At this camp there was a fence, and an old poison cart for destroying rabbits. The surroundings seemed quite home-like.

As usual, Jack and Nurie and Andy slept outside, the rest of us under the tarpaulin. Jack went up to the top of the sandridge and dug down to dry sand under a canegrass bush. Andy made himself a beautiful bed of dead buckbush with two bags on it, then his two blankets and a waterproof ground-sheet on top. It was like a thick spring mattress.

It rained gently but steadily all next day and we were confined to camp. By this time over an inch had fallen. Water was lying about everywhere on the river flat and even our sandridge was covered with little pools, mostly formed in the footprints. We had certainly chosen a remarkable season for our journey. Fortunately there was plenty of firewood. We spent most of the day reading *King Henry the Fourth* which Simpson had brought, and playing five hundred with Albert's cards.

In the afternoon Jack and Andy walked on to Annandale in the rain and reported on their return that the store was standing, with the books still in it, but the house was taken away.

Andy was pretty damp. He said the brolgas (native companions) "sing out too much - they bad animals - that frog too - all make it rain".

Next morning there was fog and mist, but the rain had stopped. Sunshine was breaking through so we packed up and got on the move once more, late in the morning. By the time we reached Annandale it was raining again and went on lightly all the rest of the day till 6.30 p.m. This time we ignored it, and carried on, a miserable procession, the camels sloshing along through mud and water.

Annandale Station was a sad ruin amid signs of former prosperity. Some outbuildings, a harness room and a store still had iron roofs on and were habitable. In the store room were a stores account book and a great bag of peppercorns. The roof and doors had been taken away from the house, but to our astonishment we found the furniture was still in it. There were beds, wardrobes, chests of drawers, a dining table, account books, garden seats, window glass, a surveyor's chain, a windmill, tools and even explosives. All were covered with dust and now subject to the ravages of wind and rain. There was a drilling plant nearby complete with boiler, casing and tools, all rusting away. The extraordinary paradox was that the waterhole by the house, half a mile long, was full of water, and the whole surroundings were choked with vegetation. Buckbush, green and luscious, had crossed the thresholds and invaded the very house, its great round masses springing up from the earthen floors in rooms that were open to the skies; but there was not a man or beast to break the desolate silence within a hundred miles. The drizzling rain added to the general depression of the scene.

Annandale was a typical example of what is often called the Kidman blight on the country, and indeed it did seem as though some plague had descended upon it, or some invader despoiled it and driven off the inhabitants. Let us look at this question a little more closely for a moment, for we are to see much more of it along the Diamantina. The Mulligan was deserted, the stations closed and all the cattle gone, yet here were water in abundance, an artesian bore half completed, and luxuriant feed for countless miles around, enough for many thousands of cattle within reach of the existing waters. How can these things be? Well, firstly, before Kidman took up the stations the previous pioneers and owners had probably failed and been forced off the holdings. We saw the river valley a maze of lakes and meadows, the bordering sandridges covered with good fodder, but this was a very exceptional season. There might not be such another, or such a succession of two or three, for another ten years. In the following summer the annual plants would die down and soon blow off the sandridges altogether; in the river flats it would wither but remain as dry fodder perhaps for another year; the water would dry up in most of the waterholes, leaving only two or three permanent waters in the whole length of the river. What the country had recently been through could be judged by the fact that not a single rabbit was to be seen along the river. The thousands of cattle that the country might carry to-day would have to be got rid of very quickly in the future. If they are not to perish they must be sold when all the neighbours are trying to find a market at the same time. It would be hard to give them away in this remote place, and they would die in thousands in the next drought. This history has repeated itself over and over again On all the private holdings in the Lake Eyre basin. Kidman's method was to take up holdings all over the vast interior, and when there were droughts in one area he could move the stock somewhere else and close the stations affected. He absorbed a great many stations in this way, and many of them are now deserted. They would probably have been deserted in any case. He could take advantage of the good seasons wherever they were, but the man on the single holding, however large, cannot do this and is ruined in a long drought. The old Cattle King is now beyond the reach of droughts and honours and curses, which all came· alike to him, but his company carries on with great success. It is the way of capital for the shareholders, and of Stalin for the people. It is the best way to make the most of our resources. There only remains the question, under which political principle is it better to carry it out?

The continuous stock-carrying capacity of any single holding in the drought areas of the interior over a long period is actually very small. It depends on the drought-resisting perennial plants like saltbush and even on the trees such as mulga, whose boughs are lopped down for the stock in times of drought. The ephemeral plants that come up in the rains are merely the fattening fodder. The permanent herbage, the mainstay of the country, is in delicate equilibrium with its surroundings, and maintains itself with difficulty even when undisturbed. The young plants are not sufficiently strong and prolific to stand up to much grazing by stock or to the attack of rabbits, so that the perennials rapidly fall away and may practically disappear. Regeneration is a slow process. The country is commonly overstocked on a new holding and eaten out to such an extent that it does not respond to the next good season, and requires a long rest before it is restored. That it does recover was abundantly shown on this journey. Kidman was accused of overstocking and ruining the country, but actually it is a question of which is better, to stock heavily for a short time and then let the country rest, or to carry a few stock continuously and never take full advantage of the good seasons. Kidman was only doing in a big way what actually happens on the individual holdings; one owner fails and goes out, another comes along after an interval and eventually fails too; but Kidman never failed because he had somewhere else to go to. Organization on Kidman's principles, and the provision of more permanent water supplies, would greatly increase our herds and flocks. The greatest problem - water - has in the past been dealt with in a very unenterprising way. Much more could be done in conserving surface water and exploiting underground water, instead of leaving it to nature to fill the few shallow waterholes she has provided. There is too much reluctance to spend money on water supply, deriving from the failure of many deep dug wells badly sited. Boring plants should entirely replace hand-sinking.

I once heard a nervous speaker trying to introduce Sir Sidney Kidman as guest of honour at a luncheon. He began with "Sir Kidney Sidman" .... and this so disconcerted him that he repeated the spoonerism and then went on to say that our guest began life as a boy of thirteen. Although such a miraculous beginning is hardly credible, the career of the old Knight was certainly a remarkable one, from those early days at Broken Hill to the position of Cattle King.

At Anndandale we refilled some of our canteens with water from the waterhole. It was "white" water, white from the fine suspended clay it carries. This was our first experience of the unpleasant white water, but we were to find it typical of the Diamantina region after rains. After this rather unnecessary supplementing of the water supply, we went on down the Mulligan valley, still travelling between high red sandridges. There was no spinifex or canegrass in the valley and it was a pleasure to be away from them. There were patches of wild lilies in places.

The river began to break up into narrow channels. About eight miles below the station it takes an offset to the west in scattered channels before continuing its old direction, and the track to Birdsville there leaves it. We passed a stockyard with windmill and tanks near here. The track had been very indistinct and beyond the stockyard we were unable to locate it at all. After a couple of miles we camped in gently rolling sandridges. Next morning we had a good look round for the track in our valley and the neighbouring ones between sandridges, but failed to find any sign of it. I had an idea that this track went round the south side of a patch of sandridges that separated us from Birdsville fifty miles away in a direct line, but it made a considerable loop to the south and would probably take a day or so longer, owing not only to the distance but also to the time wasted in finding and following it, so as we were travelling much lighter now, I decided to take to the sandridges again on a bearing of 1250 and make straight for Birdsville.

For the first few miles the sandridges were low, with sand and spinifex between them, just as in the desert, but as the day wore on they became farther apart and were separated by gibber-covered plains. The day was bitterly cold, with a south-west wind. The light load, cool weather and good feed had brought the camels back to as good condition as when they started, except that mange was spreading, and they were getting a little more difficult to manage. Most of the party were now preferring to walk. The camels had developed the habit of springing up very quickly as soon as the foot touched the stirrup to mount-a very nasty habit and liable to leave one dangling by the leg. Their defection in this direction was probably due to our bad handling.

The sandridges were now very high and separated by plains a mile or more wide. On the course we were taking it was sometimes over two miles across from ridge to ridge. In one plain there were low outcrops of sandstone, the parent of the gibbers. The gibbers in turn break down to sand and the sand is all swept up into the ridges. There was no sand at all on these stony plains, but pools of water and bogs lay about everywhere. The camels were sometimes up to their knees in water and it was difficult to pick the best way to go. Wet feet and cold wind made it a very unpleasant day.

The sandridges were as big as any we had seen. Marshall took a good strip of film of the camel string struggling across the top of one.

We had made a late start and camped late, crossing a last huge sandridge and camping well up on the far side of it, for it was too wet to make camp on the flat. The sand was wet enough, but much preferable to the mud. There was very little firewood but we were out of the wind in the lee of the sandridge. We had come seventeen miles and crossed thirteen sandridges at an acute angle.

This was most extraordinary, to come out on the edge of what is commonly thought to be and usually is a burning arid desert, and find ourselves, when not held up by rain, struggling along, freezing cold, through bogs of mud and threading our way between pools of water. We suffered from a surfeit and not a lack of water in the later stages.

It was a wonderful scene that night from our camp on the sandridge side. By nine o'clock the sky had cleared, the wind had fallen, and an almost full moon in the east was reflected from the pools and sheets of water in the plain before us. It seemed very comfortable to be in the open again after being huddled together under the tarpaulin for the last five nights of rain. Also it was only two days to Birdsville.

This sandridge seemed like a mountain range in the flat plains. I measured its height next morning and found it to be seventy-seven feet six inches. The moonlight on the water had been beautiful, but it meant a lot of wading and slogging next day. I was always rather apprehensive of bogging the camels, of which I had never had experience, but I had read a lot about losing camels along the Diamantina, and how difficult they were to de-bog. The fear of getting bogged makes the camel very nervous and this nervousness seems to infect the rider. However, most of the boggy fiats were safely crossed before the morning was over. We saw some cattle for the first time in one swampy plain, and found an emu's nest with nine eggs, some of which we had for breakfast next morning. My enjoyment of them was rather marred by seeing some bits of young emu in the omelette, which Albert was trying to pass off as normal ingredients, though why these signs of change should so put one off does not bear analysis, as it is all in the egg anyway.

In the early afternoon the orderly arrangement of sandridges and plains became broken, and a branch creek with gum trees led us down to Listore Creek, marked on the maps, which crossed our course. Beyond the creek we came into sandridges again, more like the country near the Hay, but now the sand was becoming distinctly yellower. It had lost that rich red of the desert. This meant we were at the edge of the desert and close to the Diamantina country where the sand is all light yellow. The red colour is due to a fine coating of oxide of iron (the basis of "rouge") on the grains of quartz. If boiled in acid the grains quickly become quite clear and colourless. This coating only forms under arid conditions, which is why beach sands are never red. It takes a long time to form, so that young dunes are usually white or yellow. The sandridges near the Diamantina are continually being built up from sand from the river deltas, so that the ridges are white along the river and gradually become redder towards the interior of the desert till they are as red as rouge. The same process, the solution of iron salts and their deposition by evaporation, reddens the surface of all rocks in deserts and gives them a uniform appearance. If you chip the surface away with a hammer you may find almost any colour underneath.

We were now among huge ridges up to eighty feet high and a couple of miles apart, with live sand on their crests, and separated by low and straggly twenty-foot ridges in place of the gibber plains. Once more all. was sand, and we made camp beside a miserable clump of needle bushes that provided some firewood but no shelter. There was a claypan water near by, but it was by now nothing more to us than a repulsive sight.

This was the last camp before Birdsville. We put up the wireless for the last time and sent a press message, and also had a talk to Bob Gaffney at Birdsviile. We told him we would be at the hotel at four o'clock next day. He told us the country was flooded and the mail truck was bogged on its way from Marree, so there would be no mail for us. It was uncertain when the mail would arrive. Once again it was brought home to us how reliable our ancient camel transport was. The mail was bogged and its future all unknown, but we were still poking along and would be there at four o'clock next day. The camel's time-table may show long time intervals between stations, but he runs to schedule.

The big sandridge at Andado.

12

BIRDSVILLE

LlATE got away to an early start on the next cold grey day, V" for the last seventeen miles' run, or rather slither and wade, into Birdsville. We were soon out of the sandy area and into big ridges and stony plains again. One plain was where we saw some more cattle. A boggy creek led us through the next sandridge on to a wide plain with stony undulations, almost hills, the first rises we had seen since leaving the tablelands of the Hale, the first country that was not absolutely flat plain, and in fact the last such country till Marree was reached, 400 miles away, for all our journey was in one vast plain. Away to the north-east could be seen some of the waddy trees in the patch to the north of Birdsville.

As Birdsville was approached the sandridges became close and jumbled, with small lakes that we had to go round scattered about among them. The sand was yellow, and the ridges high and hummocky. I had never approached Birdsville from this side, and few others would have done so, for I found later that we were coming down a tongue of sandridges and might have been clear of them. Four o'clock approached and there was no sign of the town, nor any indications of the proximity of one, only more sandridges in front as each one was crossed. I began to wonder if we could have passed it, though I seemed to remember that there were no sandridges anywhere near except to the west of the town. Those on foot were keeping well ahead. At last I saw them sink down on the top of the ridge ahead, tired out as i thought. When I came up beside them, there before us lay the gibber plains of Birdsville, with the few scattered tin houses shining white not half a mile away. This bare and wretched little town, the most remote in Australia, was a beautiful sight. I had been there ten years before and knew what a fascinating place it was, what generous and big-hearted people inhabited those tin dwellings among the gibbers. It looked better to me than a city with dreaming spires.

We wound down off the sandridges on to the plain. We saw a little riding party of girls and waved to them. They had come out to meet us, but shyness overcame them and they did not come close. They said afterwards that they thought the horses would be frightened of so many camels. Past the police station, and at exactly four o'clock on July 6th, the camels went down in front of the pub. There to meet us were gathered the leading citizens of Birdsville, including Norman Carralan, the policeman; Harry Afford, the hotel manager; Dorothy and Bob Gaffney, daughter and son of the proprietress; Ben Barton, the schoolmaster; and stockmen and townsmen I did not know. We took the camels to a wire yard nearby, threw off the loads, put our personal gear into Bob Gaffney's car and dumped it at the hotel again, and then, in accordance with the custom of the country, both expedition and town crowded into the little bar. We were rather. late into the bar even then I think, to satisfy the best traditions. We drank a toast to Mr. Simpson, to ourselves, to the desert, to Birdsville, and then it became a little uncertain just what toast was being drunk. After a while I withdrew from the bar and had a hot bath and a shave in anticipation of dinner at a table again, to be followed by an easy chair and a pipe before the fire and then a long sleep in a warm dry bed with sheets and a soft mattress and a roof over my head, in place of the plate on the ground, the cold wind, the damp blankets and the hard earth under a wintry sky. This is one of the greatest charms and benefits of rough living, the re-adjustment of values that makes a humble shack, a fire, and enough to eat seem all that a man could desire. Darwin said that the chief pleasure of a sea voyage was coming into port, a remark not quite so obvious to-day, but it is always true of the first few days in civilization after a primitive life in the wilderness, cut off from all the comforts and amenities that pass unnoticed in modern life. I pity all those who have never got a thrill out of switching on electric light, as we did at Birdsville. The thrill soon fades, and then it is time to think about getting away again. I remember how I resolved after two years in the Antarctic that when I got back I would never be without a block of chocolate in my pocket. Not even a start was ever made to carry out this cherished resolution. On a summer camel journey in the Sudan from Gallabat to Gedaref my drinking water was bad and always warm, and I had been without cigarettes for weeks. My mind was continually turning to thoughts of sitting in the shade at Gedaref, with a glass of cold lemon squash and a Virginian cigarette, but these. thoughts did duly and sumptuously materialize.

Marshall, our photographer.

Andy digs for a rat.

Unlike my friends in the bar, I have never been able, often to my regret, to throw off dull care and become thoroughly hilarious and hearty on a joyful occasion such as our arrival at Birdsville. The more reason for jubilation, the more sober I seem to become, while in adversity I am by comparison more stimulated and companionable. This curious reaction to success, this coldness when warmth is expected, has lost me some of the pleasures of life, even though it cloaks a deep inward satisfaction. Only Crocker joined me at the table that night. The rest remained unwashed and unfed but happy till the small hours of the morning. I joined them again for a while after dinner. The party had by then taken the form of a concert. Ben Barton was a good singer, and Albert and others were ably supporting him.

Bob Gaffney now handled our signals. He had his transmitter in the dining room, and it was a change to write a press message from Camp 25, Birdsville Hotel, sitting at a table under good light instead of on the ground out in the wind and rain. There were messages for home to be written, and acknowledgments of the many telegrams of congratulation on the successful completion of the desert crossing that were awaiting us. These things were all attended to, the pipe was smoked out, and so to bed, with greater anticipation than Pepys ever knew.

The last mail from Marree was already a week overdue.

The truck had been abandoned on the track and the driver had gone back to Marree on horseback. This was due to the rains and mud. The mail was not likely to arrive for at least another week. The weather was still very cold and windy, with occasional rain, and we decided to layoff in Birdsville for a few days till the country had dried up somewhat and the movements of the mail were known. We were out of moving picture film and had very little still picture film left, but otherwise were not in need of supplies. There was more film in the mail truck. The future plans of the expedition could wait a few days.

There was to have been a reception ball on our arrival but the people had not been able to come in from the surrounding stations owing to the state of the country, and it was quite indefinite when this would be possible. However, there were other social duties, and entertainments not to be neglected or missed; it was out of the question to think of moving on till this lonely little town had given us the honour and hospitality it was so glad to offer. My experience of ten years before, on the aerial reconnaissance, when aeroplanes had landed there for the first time, had taught me what to expect and what was expected. Then the country was in a desperate plight through being in the end of a long drought. The cattle were all dying and the few horses that were left could not travel, so that the people who did not have motor cars had to come in by camel. Now it was floods and bogs that kept them away. The people at Birdsville were interested then in my desert investigations, and had followed this expedition with even greater interest. They had lived their lives on the edge of the desert and understood the difficulties of crossing it. Their congratulations meant more to us than all the generous expressions of those who did not know. I was very much at home here.

On our first day in, Birdsville we made a tour of calls at all the homes in the town - about six - under the conductorship of Norman Carralan. No one who was at home was neglected. We also visited the school and the Australian Inland Mission Hostel. One old lady who had some pretty young daughters who were much in demand, told us of her first journey up from New South Wales in a waggonette. Another had a nice little garden, with ripe tomatoes, onions, nasturtiums, and oranges. Her son was droving cattle to Marree and the mob was just passing through Birdsville. We expected to catch up to him near Goyder's Lagoon and get some meat, as he would be killing there. We saw the well-borer who had worked on the Annandale bore, with his wife and pretty little daughter. It was rather remarkable that we should find a crop of half a dozen attractive young girls blossoming in so small a patch of the desert - surely as rare a state of affairs as the good seasons themselves. Their sweetness was not wasted on the party, and it all helped towards a gay and happy stay.

It was tea time when the last call was made, and a little boy had to be brought in to have his hot dinner in front of us. He was very shy, and we so overwhelmed him with our attentions that he sat at the table and cried into his bowl of soup. His rather grubby little baby sister on the other hand thought it was a great occasion, and clapped and laughed.

The A.I.M. had moved out of the hotel that had been their quarters and were in new buildings. There were two sisters - Henderson and McKenzie - and their hostel was the social centre of the place, in the best traditions of the A.I.M., and as it used to be in Alice Springs.

At the school next day we found a few black children under a bough shelter outside, and a few white children in the main building. I gave them a talk on our journey, with the aid of a map, and then paid some special attention to the little blacks outside. The native children get along very quickly in the early stages at school and up to a certain point. They are very good with their fingers and make beautiful figures in their sums. They recited for us "Two little kittens one stormy night, began to quarrel and then to fight. One had a mouse and the other had none, and that was how the quarrel begun". They said it very rapidly in a soft monotone, with their heads down so that we could hardly follow it. Ben Barton said he had a hard job to teach them this recitation. They had only just started school and it was one of the first things they had learnt. They got the idea all right but were not particular about the exact form of the words. One of them favoured "Two little scats, big stormy fight". Another said "Two little kittens, big rain jump up." None of them would say "the other had none" but always "the other had no mouse." To celebrate the occasion I gave the school a half- holiday which is the only really memorable and impressive thing to do when visiting a school. I had no authority to do this, but even if I had made it a week's holiday I do not think it would have been likely to reach the ears of the education authorities in Brisbane.

The black children spent their lunch time sitting on the wood-heap at the hotel, where Mrs. Gaffney would give them food. It was hard to get them away from the wood-heap till Barton instituted a bell, but after that they would all come back at the run when he rang it. They called it the dindle, for obvious reasons, as it was a cattle bell.

In the afternoon there was a grand riding party. Norman Carralan provided horses for the whole expedition. He had some police horses and in addition a number of drovers' horses that passing drovers had left in his care. The local girls and the sisters had their usual mounts and we made an imposing cavalcade, with quite a sprinkling of blood stock, for this was a country of good horses. It was a wonderful change from our camel riding. The ground was very heavy, but we scrambled down to the river and splashed across shoulder deep in the fast-running water, and then downstream till we overtook a drover with a thousand heifers making for New South Wales. He had spent a night at the hotel, a big man muffled up in a huge greatcoat, with muddy boots and spurs, and a camera slung across his shoulder, none of which he removed at the table or at any time as far as I knew, for I never saw him without them. I asked him about the camera and he said he always kept it handy to snap any unusual scene, the sort of thing that there is no time .to go and get a camera for, like cattle breaking, or swimming rivers, and he used to send the pictures to the press.

It was the height of the droving season, and owing to the recent good seasons there were plenty of cattle to move. Half a dozen mobs were within a day or two's distance of Birdsville, and the drovers were making the best of their opportunities while within reach of the place, for the next stop is Marree, over three weeks away. In the palmy days there used to be seven hotels in Birdsville, but now they were reduced to one. Men were in great demand at this time and the drovers, the professional full-time drovers who own a plant and hire assis¬tants, were having a difficulty in holding their men. His two men deserted old Greatcoat next day and returned to the hotel. I often wondered how he got on about it. It is quite a usual thing for a drover to have to fight his men to induce them to stay on. The extraordinary thing about it is that if the man loses the fight he seems quite willing to stay. The idea seems to be that the boss is then shown to be a good man to work for.

When I asked one drover about his difficulties he made a very wise remark that applies to leaders in all walks of life, and I have often quoted it since. He said a drover must know more than his men and do more than his men. It was said of old Greatcoat that he lay under his blankets in the morning and expected his men to get the cattle on the move without him.

On the way back from the cattle we had a race over a wide and rather boggy flat. It seemed dangerous to me and I noticed that Carralan had more respect for his mount and stayed behind. It was a wild gallop of a mile or more through the mud. I expected a fall and a broken leg or two and did not think the horses could stand up to it, but they breed them hardy up there. One of the girls won, on a little black blood mare.

The hostel entertained us that night. It was an extension of the usual weekly gathering. There was ping-pong, at which Bob Gaffney beat all comers, and an impromptu concert, and a wonderful supper of dainties cooked by the sisters. Everyone was present, including the passing drovers. The children sat on the floor round the room with their backs to the walls.

It began to be harder to stand up to the hospitality of Birdsville than to trek across the desert.

The next day was a Sunday. Some of us went out by car to the waddy trees in the stony ground about four miles to the north of Birdsville and on the west side of a low tableland. We collected seed and made notes on the tree, confirming that it was the same tree as we had seen at the Andado Bore No.1. At Birdsville it grows within an area of a square mile at most and is an isolated occurrence.

On our return I had a look at the local rock formations, which consist of some small and low sandstone and conglomerate outcrops near the town, the only solid rock to be found for many miles around.

In the afternoon there was a cricket match, town plus drovers against expedition plus drovers, in which the expedition won by a narrow margin. Bob Gaffney and Crocker both retired at twenty-four, and Jack Bejah took the hat trick. While this was going on I took the opportunity of getting down to the plans for the future. The main object of the expedition had been achieved, and a mail truck would soon be going back to Marree which could take us in to the railway in a few days; but the camels had to return to Marree and although it would take a month longer I did not want to miss the opportunity of going down the river and seeing Lake Eyre after the rains, to compare conditions with what I had seen ten years before after a long drought. It was four hundred and fifty miles to Marree via the lake, and would take a good four weeks by camel, whereas the mail would do the three hundred and sixty miles down the track in three days when the state of the track allowed it to continue its running. I decided not to wait for the uncertain mail truck, but to go on down the Diamantina to Lake Eyre by camel with a reduced party, leaving Birdsville on Tuesday, July 11th. Marshall had no film for further photography, and the press did not want any more messages now that the excitement was over, so that the wireless could be dispensed with. I was by this time rather worried about the way mange was spreading among the camels and we had no treatment for it. We did not need to carry much water, so that loads could be considerably reduced and we could travel lighter and faster. Simpson and Marshall would remain at Birdsville for the mail, and bring on the wireless gear, cameras, six canteens and the botanical and biological specimens already collected, and the rest of us would go on by camel. I checked stores and ordered what was wanted, chiefly a few things in Albert's department.

The next day would be our last in Birdsville, and we would leave the following morning, for it seemed that the hospitality of Birdsville would never exhaust itself. It had by this time almost exhausted me, and I was feeling the need of some restful travelling again.

Every morning at eight o'clock Bob Gaffney sat at his pedal set in the dining room contacting all the stations in his range from far away in Queensland through the north-east of South Australia and down the track to Marree. This was a regular arrangement when everybody stood by to exchange news. It made them all one family, a round-the-table conference of people many hundreds of miles apart. The news was all local and domestic- illnesses, visitors, who was on the track, where the cattle were, how the mail was getting along, when Bill or Harry were expected in, what the track was like and how the rains were going. What was happening in the outside world had practically no interest at all for them and it seemed that no one ever listened to national stations. It was a little world of its own. "All O.K., Bob, all O.K.". "Well, I don't think we have anything else here, Peter, I don't think we have anything else here. So over to you, Peter, over to you" - or "Over to you, Sister, over to you".

A story typical of outback humour was told of Albert Blinman from Glengyle, who at the time was a willing slave at the Hostel. It is a perfect example of the pleasant answer and the bushman's optimism. Bob and Albert were trying to knock a leaf of a spring back into place, and Albert was under the car, Bob banging away in an awkward position with hammer and chisel. The spring had about three inches to go. After about ten minutes Bob asked how it was going and Albert answered enthusiastically, "Oh, she's going by leaps and bloody bounds!" When it was Bob's turn to get under he found it had moved about half an inch.

That day I made a more critical study of the river in the vicinity. The banks are of clay, but most of the bed was covered with running water. There was sand and gravel at some of the bends, but I was told that gravelly places were rare. Bob Gaffney had found a diprotodon jaw near the town and I wanted to see his locality and to make a further search. The Diamantina is a well-known locality for the remains of these extinct giant wombats, as well as of giant kangaroos and emus. The search for fossil bones was one of my objects in going down the river, but it proved hopeless as we found the river was quite full lower down. Even at Birdsville there was too much water to see much of the river bed and I found some calcified roots, like Leichhardt's bones, but Bob's diprotodon jaw was genuine, and a good specimen. He still had it at the house.

The local sandridges came in for further examination too.

Birdsville is on the west side of the river, and the origin and beginning of sandridges can be seen here. It can be observed that they advance across the gibber plains in the direction of their length. It is to be noted that they are referred to as ridges, not dunes. Dunes are crescent-shaped and lie across the direction of the wind and move sideways. These ridges are parallel to the prevailing winds, and extend by growing onwards at their ends, creeping forward lengthways like a snake. This advance over the clean-swept gibbers is shown at the end of every ridge by the fan of fresh sand enveloping bushes and shrubs. At the other end, the south-east end, the ridge is worn away, the cane grass bushes once growing on the ridge now left standing on pillars of sand held together by the roots. The side-winds play an important part in ridge development, and shape the crests where the sand is live. There are often small dunes on top of the ridges. The stronger winds are from the south-west, which gives the gentler slope on the west side of the ridges and the steeper slope formed by falling sand on the east. East winds may reverse the slopes in the live sand on the crests. This was often seen in the Birdsville area, where there were sometimes steep banks on the western side of the crests, but it was never observed west of the Hay.

The dance could be deferred no longer, so it was arranged for our last night. Only one party decided to try to get in from outside the town. They were Mr. and Mrs. Leo Crabb from Pandi Pandi down the Diamantina in South Australia the station where the sandridge crept up from the south and went between the kitchen and the living quarters and separated them so that the occupants had to climb over the ridge on a wire netting track every time they wanted to go from one place to the other. The Crabbs were to arrive early in the afternoon by car and Bob Gaffney made several trips to the punt to see if they were waiting to come over the river. By sundown it was obvious that they had struck trouble, so the policeman sent a tracker and horses out to help them. He found their car bogged and brought them back, wet, exhausted, and covered with mud; and to crown her troubles, Mrs. Crabb's case had been dropped off the packhorse in the darkness somewhere on the way in, probably in the river at the crossing. She had nothing to change into, but the women came to the rescue most effectively and satisfactorily, and Mrs. Crabb soon warmed up after her late start. She was the lady who ten years before had said, on leaving for home after the dance, "That was good-oh; it will do me for another year". Leo himself did not put in an appearance at the dance till considerably later.

Ten years ago a man had played an accordion right through the dance practically without stopping, though it must be admitted that liquor as well as the ideal of service to others had something to do with that feat of endurance. Now there was a gramophone with electric pick-up, another activity of that progressive and active young man, Bob Gaffney. Ten years ago water reticulation pipes had been laid down in the town for five years past, but the river level had not risen high enough to fill the lagoon that was to supply the system and it had not been used. Now the raised tank was full, but leaking, and had made a bog on the track to the Council. Chamber, which was the ballroom. A hurricane lamp was hung at this bog as a warning, but Albert took it for a street lamp to light the way and made straight for it, and was bogged to the knees.

The dance was a great success. Everyone was there, even the babies, which were asleep in beds provided for the purpose in a room at the back. A young silent-heeler cattle dog enjoyed himself immensely. He ran round the edge of the floor, or sat up with eyes sparkling, and snapped at the dancers' heels as they went by. He did a bit of damage to one girl, but gave up when the trooper caught him a back kick in the face. There was no drink and no sitting out. Partners separated as soon as each dance was over. Drinking and love-making are taken seriously and separately in the outback, where men are still men and not gigolos; each has its proper time and place, where it can be enjoyed in a big way, but a dance is definitely not the time or place for either.

In the small hours of the morning Leo Crabb made a speech of welcome to the expedition, and every member responded except poor old Andy, who was not officially there, though he probably got his share of the supper, which, incidentally, would have done credit to any entertainment.

Another grey dawn was beginning to spread over the gibber plains when the happy party broke up.

13

DOWN THE DIAMANTINA

TO cross the Simpson Desert had been the main object of the expedition, and that had been achieved. We now started on quite a different phase, the return to Marree through the flood-plains of the Diamantina. This part of the journey was in known country most of which had been occupied at one time or another and was trigonometrically surveyed and roughly mapped. Still, it is very remote and unusual country, full of interest, romance and tragedy, about which little has been written, so we will continue the story of our travels till the camels are let loose again on the Common at Marree.

Difficulties and uncertainties had given a spirit of adventure to the desert crossing, but actually the daily routine was terribly monotonous, with the same endless sandridges day after day. By comparison, the remainder of the journey was full of natural interest and variety. Usually the Birdsville track is a drought-stricken desert, but we were to see it under very exceptional conditions, with the river running and the desert blooming. Our plan now was to continue the biological and botanical collecting round this fringe of the desert, as well as to see just what became of the waters of the Diamantina, which had been running for some months, to re-examine Lake Eyre and find out whether these two exceptionally wet seasons had put any water into it, and to search the river bed for fossil remains of the extinct animals that roamed these plains in former pluvial times. The exceptional season made it a wonderful opportunity for natural history collecting.

Lake Eyre is the focus of an enormous inland drainage system, stretching from the MacDonnells in Central Australia to the Dividing Range in Queensland and covering half a million square miles of country. The main streams are the Finke and the Macumba from the north-east, and the Diamantina and the Cooper from the north-east, each of them many hundreds of miles long. Most of them run only at rare intervals and their floods seldom reach the lake. The Cooper has not run in its lower courses since 1917. It has countless lakes and swamps to fill on its way. The Diamantina runs at Birdsville almost every year, but usually only a "channel flood" not inundating the country, such a run as was now on. It would be interesting to see how far the water went.

To the north of the Lake lie the waterless sandridges of the Simpson Desert, but to the east and north-east stretch hundreds of miles of the flood plains of the Diamantina and Cooper, with countless lakes and claypans, scattered stony plains, and fewer but often higher sandridges.

The rain had now ceased and the surface water was drying up, but strong and bitterly cold winds were constantly blowing. We had little more actual wading through water like we had experienced on the way in to Birdsville, but travelling was for the most part damp, cold and miserable. Fortunately the wind invariably died down at six o'clock and the nights were calm.

We got away from Birdsville after lunch on July 11th, waving farewell to all our friends and facing into a bleak wind for the start of our four hundred mile journey to the railway. There is a signpost in Birdsville with three arms reading, "Marree 330 miles, Bedourie 125 miles, Betoota 108 miles". Those are the nearest places along the three tracks leading out of the town. Only Marree is of importance; the other two are only little Queensland centres like Birdsville. There can be few places in the world where the next village is over a hundred miles away.

We made seven miles south that afternoon and camped on a small sandridge in South Australia, just across the border fence. Once more the sky was our roof and sand or buckbush our bed.

We intended to use the Birdsville-Marree stock and mail route, "The Birdsville Track", as far as it went down the Diamantina, and where it left the river we would leave it and continue on down the river to the lake. There are alternative routes at the top end of the track. The fine-weather track keeps to, the west of the river, the same side as Birdsville is on, as far as Goyder's Lagoon, which it crosses at the far end opposite the ruins of the old station of that name, and there it joins the wet-weather track which lies entirely on the east side of the river, and is reached by crossing the Diamantina in the punt at Birdsville. We chose the shorter fine-weather trail. The first objective was the great Andrewilla Waterhole about forty miles below Birdsville and near the head of Goyder's Lagoon. The track runs south from Birdsville along the· edge of the Diamantina flood-plain and then turns into it along the course of a tributary, the Eleanor, which leads down to the waterhole. We were travelling in flat country but passing the ends, or rather the beginnings, of the sandridges of the desert on our right' all the way to the Eleanor. They were high ridges, sixty feet or so, and of yellow sand, rather pale and harmless-looking after the fierce red ridges of the Interior; in fact they were even friendly, as they were dry to camp on, made better going for the camels, and were covered with good feed. It was now the wet and muddy plains that were forbidding.

Simpson and Marshall, with a riding party, were to overtake us near the fence next day, but we did not 'see them; again it was a case of the stern chase of a camel proving unexpectedly long, There were several waterholes along the track, usually situated near the end of a sandridge. We passed the Dickerrie and the Eight Mile, and camped on the Karrathunka Waterhole on the Eleanor, an indefinite stream which appears to connect up the waterholes. There we nearly overtook Tom Finlay, a drover with a mob of cattle who had given us fifty pounds of meat at Birdsville. We saw two of his men on their horses on the crest of a sandridge beyond our camp. The cattle were the other side and out of sight. Apparently they were not going to camp yet. They stood for a long time and watched us make camp, lonely black figures silhouetted against the grey and wintry sky. It was a cold, hard, comfortless time for them. I was reminded of the dingoes staring down on our desert camps. Then they disappeared. I thought if they camped soon they would come back to us, but we never saw them again.

Next day we went on .down the Eleanor, which became merely a strip of flooded country between sandridges, with occasional waterholes. The waterholes were full, but there was by this time little surface water lying about and we had no difficulty with the camels, except for mud in a few channels. At a big waterhole, the Ten Mile, we found a boomerang marked with the names of a party of drovers, Hayes' party, who were well ahead of us, and a little later another party passed us on their way back to Queensland for more cattle. These men were in a hurry. Fifteen miles a day is about ·the rate for travelling with stock, but without them the drover travels fast, covering perhaps, fifty miles in a day, a rate quite out of the camel's class. The drover has very high heels to his elastic-sided boots, to prevent his feet from slipping through the stirrups. Hard and permanent cones of grey clay had formed on these men's heels, making them even longer. I wondered how they managed to walk in them at all, not that the horseman does walk very much. Incidentally, the elastic sides are to help the foot to slip out of the boot in the case of being thrown and dragged by the stirrup.

Near the Diamantina the course of the Eleanor became much more river-like, with high box gums, and the feed, which had been scant further back, grew most luxuriously. There were giant buckbushes, spherical masses five feet or more across. This is the rolypoly, common throughout the drier parts of Australia. It is lightly anchored to the soil by its roots and when dead breaks away and bowls across the country before the wind for miles. Where there are fences they become piled high with it so that the bushes are soon rolling over the top. It is good camel and cattle feed when green... There was saltbush and parrot flower, and on the sandridges great stretches of wild stocks in bloom, making a wonderful show. In some places we saw new plants coming up in such profusion that the whole surface of the sand was pocked with the little crusty pieces raised up on the stems below.

Near the end of the Eleanor we came upon a great pile of stores covered with a tarpaulin, groceries of all kinds and material for Clifton Hills Station, evidently left there because the truck bringing them, could not get across the Diamantina. There were no signs of any track. We left a message written on a board.

The last sandridge along the Eleanor was measured and found to be eighty feet high.

We made camp on the side of the Andrewilla Waterhole, a permanent water up to two hundred yards across and several miles long. This water is at the eastern end of Goyder's Lagoon, a plain fifty miles long by fifteen miles wide, over which the Diamantina spreads in countless small lignum-lined gutters which reunite again below into a single channel and then again divide into two parts, the Warburton and the Kallakoopah, before reaching Lake Eyre. Between the lagoon and Birdsville the river is made up of several channels and swamps but above Birdsville there is again only a single well-defined channel.

We decided to spend a day at this waterhole. There were the ruins of a mud hut which had been a police station in the days when blacks were numerous. All that are left of these tribes are now either in Birdsville or Marree, or on the few stations that still survive. The white man dispossessed the black, and now he too is driven out and the country is deserted. Andy himself was a survivor. He told some grisly tales of a certain policeman with a Hunnish name who used to shoot the blacks and then lay them out in rows and poke them with a burning stick to see if they were still alive, for it was a common trick to pretend to be dead. What truth there was in this I do not know, but Andy believed it. He said the proper name of the waterhole was Annarrawilla.

I had brought fishing lines, and early in the morning Albert went fishing with cockatoo's gut, which he said was good bait. He had lived for some time on the Murray. It was not long before he came running up with several carp, weighing a pound or two each, and soon we were all fishing. One fish was put in spirit, but the rest made an excellent dinner of fish and chips. The water in the hole, like all the claypan water, was opaque white and the fish were a curious dead white colour too. We naturally thought that these fishes, being common in the Diamantina, would be well known to science, so we only preserved one, which was determined later by the Australian Museum as *Hephaestus welchi*, known only by the single type specimen taken at Innamincka on the Cooper, which suggests that there is still work to be done on the fishes in the Inland waters.

The trees were alive with cockatoos. Birdsville got its name from the flocks of birds that frequent this part of the river.

I watched a very wonderful dawn at this waterhole, one that has stood out clearly in my memory ever since, among the hundred dawns we saw. It was cloudless and calm. I lay in my bed on the bare ground above the steep bank, just beyond the thin line of trees that edged the waterhole. The moon was high, but its light was already paling and the shadows were gone. Orion still rode the skies, but the glorious morning star in the east was heralding the approach of the bold sun. The sky still held the dark blue of the night, but towards the east it changed to dove grey, then light grey and finally to a strip of tangerine that lay low on the horizon. They were not the brilliant colours of sunset clouds, but the most delicate hues of the sky itself. The black trees were silhouetted against these lovely tints. Gradually the stars faded and the mystic moonlight withdrew as night crept silently away, and objects took their true shape and distance in the hard light of day. A squawk was heard here and there in the trees, and soon the clouds of cockatoos came to life and filled the morning with their harsh screeching, tearing away the last soft trailing veils of night as the sun came up.

We packed up and got away from the waterhole. Adventure was not quite gone from the journey, for there was likely to be trouble with bogs, and Goyder's Lagoon was an obstacle that was causing us some apprehension. Even the southern track is not always passable, but the mail had been using it for some time, abandoning the considerably shorter northern track that crosses the lagoon, as the lagoon becomes quite impassable to vehicles as soon as the river runs, owing not so much to the mud as to the depth of the gutters themselves. Accounts varied about the state of the lagoon. Cattle were still following that track, but whether loaded camels could get through was another thing. Some drovers said the water was still rising, some that it was falling. I had decided to risk it, but it was going to be very awkward if we could not get across, and even worse if we got half the team bogged.

We continued on westward along the edge of Goyder's Lagoon plain, passing the ends of the desert sandridges. There was a good deal of open water and some boggy ground, but so far the going was fair. At noon we came to the long Pelican Waterhole, where there were a lot of ducks. I shot three but could only recover one as the wind blew the others out of reach.

During the afternoon we saw ahead a large circular disc like a notice board, stuck up on the end of a sandridge. When we arrived at it we found it was the end of a forty-gallon petrol drum of a familiar yellow colour, that had been cut out of the drum. There were other ends lying about, with holes in them where smaller discs had been cut out, and the tracks of a truck were still clear. So this was where the Birdsville mailman on his last trip on this route had cut clutch plates out of petrol drums to repair his ruined clutch! We had read about it in the newspapers, but though I have the greatest respect for the ingenuity of the bush mechanic, I had thought this was going a bit too far in good stories. However, here was proof of it. Hammer, cold chisel and file were probably his only tools.

After a short day of fifteen miles we reached Burt's Waterhole, a small temporary hole in a gutter, full of thick white water. As mentioned before, this white water is characteristic of the lower Mulligan and Diamantina plains. It is due to a fine white clay in suspension in the water. As the water dries up it becomes thicker till it reaches a gelatinous stage and finally only dry grey clay remains. We saw a horse plant approaching the waterhole from the opposite direction, and hurried in to get first choice of camping ground, but the others made for a place in the open a few hundred yards down the ditch. I went down later to see them and soon found the reason for this. The water in the hole was too thick to use, but in. the ditch it was comparatively clear. They had been there before. I found it was Hayes, whose party had inscribed the boomerang. His two men had left him in Marree and he was going back with a blackfellow, Sandy, and a new hand, for another mob of cattle from Durrie on the river above Birdsville.

Burt's Waterhole was on the edge of the sandhills, with a few sorry-looking trees in the vicinity. This was the last timber before Goyder's Lagoon Waterhole twenty-five miles away across the lagoon, according to Jack, who had travelled this part of the track before, so we made up some loads of faggots to carry with us.

After we had finished our meal, the other party visited us.

Hayes reported a lot of water on the lagoon plain, which he had just crossed, and seemed rather doubtful of our succeeding in getting over with the camels. He did not think the mail truck would be able to get in to Goyder's Lagoon old station but would have to go round it, so we would miss our mail. It had been arranged that if the mail got through in time they were. to leave our letters in the old building on their return.

It turned out that Sandy was a friend of Andy's and the two of them had a great yarn. It was soon clear that they wanted Andy to join them, and rather to my surprise I found that Andy wanted to go. We ourselves were heading for home and comfort, and would have needed some very strong inducement to turn back and retrace our steps over the same dull and muddy trail. I never knew what sort of home or ties Andy had in Marree, but here he was, willing in a moment to turn his back on them and start all over again on the track we were so glad to leave behind us. It brought it strongly home that there was really no discomfort at all for him in this life, that he was at home all the time on the long walkabout, and happier here than in the hovels round a town. Next morning Andy was still of the same mind, so I reluctantly decided to let him go. He was really in Jack's employ; and Jack too was willing. I gave him six ounces of tobacco and an expedition mug as a souvenir, and promised him any clothing he wanted at Scobie's store in Marree when he should reach there again. And so we said good-bye to Andy. He had made a great contribution to the expedition with his keen collecting; he had been a tireless worker about the camp, and not least, he had been a constant source of interest and amusement with his quaint and eager ways and his myths and native lore. I had become very fond of Andy, and was disappointed that he should want to leave me, but I made no move to dissuade him. It was best for him. Our journey would be over in another three weeks.

Actually we suspected there was some heart interest in it for Andy, for he told us that a gin at Birdsville, Lucy, was all the time looking at him there, the last remark of Andy's that stays in my mind.

Hayes told us that McAuley with his cattle was only just ahead of us. We hoped to catch him up at about Mt. Gason Bore, and get the promised meat.

We had now to tackle the Goyder's Lagoon crossing. At Dead Man sandridge, six miles beyond Burt's Hole over grey flats, we left the sandridge margin and went into the plain. The next landmark was One Tree, seven miles away, an isolated tree in the plains. Before we reached it we began to cross gutters. We crossed a dozen in the next five miles. They were from ten to thirty feet across, and running full, the water only an inch or two below the surface of the level ground. The depth was usually only up to the camels' knees, but one could never tell what the bottom would be like, or the depth. We generally avoided the places where the cattle had crossed, as being likely to be more cut up and boggy, but on the other hand they were probably the best and shallowest places. My camel, Snowy, was the best trained and most experienced, and he would face up to it, so I went over first and the string followed. There was some staggering and splashing, but as one ditch after another was safely crossed we began to gain more confidence. The plain was covered with vegetation, high marsh-mallows along the ditches, and a carpet of yellow daisies and billy-buttons all around. The ditches were lined with the dreary swamp lignum but it all appeared to be dead.

We camped in the lagoon on the hard ground only a few inches above the level of the water, and made a fire from our load of wood. Three ducks settled on the water near the camp but were off again before fire could be brought to bear on them. During the day we had seen dotterel, a few quail, and some hawks.

The lagoon had been a bugbear, but we were now more than half way across it and there were only another six miles to go.

A man with horses from Cowarie Station passed us on the plain. He said he was going to Birdsville, and asked us if we had seen any stray cattle about. We got the impression that he was looking for lonely cattle that wanted a home.

We crossed more gutters next morning and soon the low stony tableland on the far side of the lagoon came into view. Half a mile before we reached it we entered a cane grass swamp almost covered with water, and the going became very difficult. Even Snowy was making heavy weather of it. Nurie on his light young camel forged ahead and soon stood waiting for us on the dry land. Progress was very slow. The pack camels sank to their knees in the mud at every step, and it was as much as they could do to drag each foot out again. Jack shouted and urged, and the string crept slowly on. I heard the steady flock-flock-flock behind me as the feet came out of the deep holes they had made, and dreaded to hear it cease, for to stop in the mud is fatal. The gap between us and the shore diminished with exasperating slowness, but at last we stood with Nurie on the firm ground. It took exactly fifty-five minutes to cover the last half mile.

The Goyder's Lagoon Waterhole was some way off on our right among trees, but we had seen more than enough of water. We went up the slight rise on to a gibber plain and soon joined the track from the waterhole to the old station five miles away. There was more mud and water round the station, which we found to be nothing but ruined mud walls with the exception of an open iron-roofed shed with a fire-place at one end. We found no signs of the mail having been there, so we left a note saying we had passed on and would keep to the track as far as Mt. Gason Bore.

There was a long narrow waterhole near the station and it was literally swarming with ducks swimming up and down, many of them young but full grown, and so unafraid that one could walk up within twenty yards of them. I got out the gun. It was a duck shooter's dream. Once they rose they flew up and down, over the water, passing the same point again and again. I stood by the trunk of a gum tree and brought down ten, and only stopped to conserve ammunition. The ducks settled again and Crocker shot another five. There was every kind of duck, black duck, widgeon, teal, and a big brown duck I had never seen before. Marshall got a good moving picture of them at the same spot later on.

As we were leaving the old station we had our first bog, in the gutter running away from this waterhole, a ditch only a few feet across. The camel had to be unloaded, but eventually struggled out itself. The remains of our dried fruits and the tea had got soaked. The tea later turned to solid blocks in its packets and went rather mouldy.

Soon after, we saw a truck bogged on the plain, and found it was the mail, with the driver and one passenger, bound for Birdsville. They were soon out of that trouble, but anxious to push on to the higher ground on the other side of the station, for all about there the ground was treacherous, and though it did not appear to have rained for several days, I noticed that water had just arrived there and was spreading and extending before our eyes. I was anxious to get on better ground myself, so it was arranged that we should proceed a mile or two to a tree by a waterhole and they should try to get past the station, and when we had each got out of our difficulties we would meet again. We discussed opening the mailbags, which was irregular, but the mailman was inclined to agree to it; in fact he suggested it, but we postponed a final decision till later.

We camped early at this One Tree camp - Camp 31 for us - to keep near the mail. There were more ducks on this ¬waterhole, and I had another unusual duck-shooting experience. Under cover of some bushes, and with much crawling in mud, I reached the side of the hole with a small-bore rifle. The ducks were more scared here and remained on the far side of the hole about fifty yards away, swimming slowly along. They were not more than a hundred yards from our camp in the open, where men and camels were still moving about, I shot four ducks with five shots, and the remarkable thing was that the wind was blowing directly across the water and blew the ducks one by one right into my hands as I lay there on the edge. We had all the ducks we wanted by then and there was no point in going on shooting. We each had three or four to pluck and just got them finished in daylight. Albert cooked a dinner of roast duck, green peas and potatoes. It was hard to say which was most memorable, the turkey on the Hay, the fish and chips at Andrewilla Waterhole, or the roast duck at Goyder's Lagoon. It was lucky we still had some of our load of firewood for there was no other wood about. Again we were camped on damp ground only a few inches above the level of the water in the hole. There was no further sign of the mailman and his passenger that night.

In the morning Jack took Snowy and went to look for the mail truck. He followed their track for about five miles, and only turned back when the going got much better. He said the truck had been bogged near the old station but had got away and gone on beyond reach. Jack and Albert had both thought they heard a truck in the morning, so it had not been far away that night. We felt that the mailman had let us down. However, with any luck they would overtake us on their way back in a few days. We would keep to the track as far as Mt. Gason bore, or five miles to the south of it, where there was said to be a letterbox belonging to Mona Downs, a new station across the Warburton opposite that point on the track.

I now decided to go to this station and have a look at the Warburton and Kallakoopah, and then follow the Warburton down to Lake Eyre, calling at Cowarie Station, which had been reoccupied. As we were now unlikely to catch up to the drovers ahead, we would be short of meat, and must get some at Mona Downs or Cowarie.

There are artesian bores all along the Marree-Birdsville track from Goyder's Lagoon downwards, at intervals of about twenty-five miles, to provide water for the stock route. They are at Goyder's Lagoon, Mt. Gason, Mira Mitta, Mungeranie, Mulka, Kopperamanna, Dulcaninna, the Clayton and Lake Harry. They are all flowing bores, with the water practically boiling. It was only a few miles from the old station to Goyder's Lagoon bore, and we had been looking forward for some time to having hot baths there. The track here follows along the indented front of the low rise that separates the river flats from the surrounding plains. The flats were boggy and water was still running down on to them from the higher ground in little streams at intervals along the scarp. It was only just arriving and spreading near the old station, which was in a bay in the flats. We soon left the flats and went up to the better going on the plains, which we found were covered with gibbers. Sturt crossed Goyder's Lagoon in a dry time and did not associate it with any river. He came back quite unaware of the existence of the Diamantina. He called the gibber plains in the north-east corner of South Australia the Stony Desert. There are no particular geographical boundaries to Sturt's Stony Desert. It is merely the part he visited of the vast area of similar gibber plains that make up a big proportion of the Lake Eyre Basin.

The reader may know, or have already gathered by inference, what gibbers are, but in case there is any doubt remaining, it may be said that gibbers are flat, roundish and flinty pebbles of all sizes from an inch or two across up to six inches or more. They are dark red to yellow in colour and are smoothed by sand-blast and even quite polished through a coating of "desert varnish", a deposit of colloidal silica or oxide of iron, or both, which is a characteristic superficial process in hot and arid regions. They are formed through the breaking up of an old siliceous or flinty soil horizon, formed possibly in more pluvial times, from which the wind has removed the loose soil cover. Solid siliceous crusts still cap the table-topped hills and preserve them, while round about the crust has been broken up and the softer underlying beds removed by wind and water erosion, but still the crust remains as a red carpet of gibbers on the surface. Larger masses of the old crust are called "billy" in Queensland.

The gravelly gibber plains are similar to the reg and serir of the Sahara, where the table-tops are called hammada, but our gibbers are smoother and rounder than the stones of most deserts. The word is pronounced with a hard "g". Its origin appears to be unknown, though some aboriginal source is probable.

The bore stream at Goyder's Lagoon runs into a creek which was swampy at the time, and there were the usual flocks of ducks on it, of which I got another five, and clouds of noisy cockatoos. There were box gums and water plants along the creek but the bore was several hundred yards to the side on the bare gibber plain. Over half a million gallons of boiling water pours out of the bore day in and day out, and runs down a gutter to the creek. The gutter is fenced for the first couple of hundred yards to keep the stock off it till it has had time to spread and cool. On the lower ground there was a grove of big acacias which made a very pleasant camping place, with the hot stream flowing past the door. In this winter weather a cloud of steam could be seen over the bores from many miles away. There were gravelly pools surrounded by green grasses and for a bath it was just a matter of walking along till you found a pool at a temperature that suited you, and then sitting down in it. Instead of the three stages of the Roman baths, there was an infinite range for warming-up or cooling off. The bathing was

Andy loads a groaning camel.

Preparing to go.

particularly delightful in this cold weather.

Goyder's Lagoon bore was put down in 1905 to a depth of 4,850 feet. It delivered when first completed 600,000 gallons a day at a temperature of 208°F. and a pressure of 173 pounds per square inch at the surface. The dissolved salts amounted to 56 grains to the gallon, which is very low for artesian basin water, the figure in South Australia being usually nearer 200 grains to the gallon. The limit for human beings to live on is placed at about 300 grains to the gallon, and sea water contains over 2,000 grains to the gallon. The bores along the Birdsville track give much better water than the mound springs and bores round the margin of the basin. The salts in the waters are characterized by the high percentage of soda compared with lime or magnesia. In Goyder's Lagoon bore water, 41 out of the 56 grains of solids are carbonate of soda, and eight grains are common salt. The salts consist usually of common salt the most, then carbonate of soda, followed by sulphate of soda, carbonate of magnesia, and carbonate of lime, with variable sulphate of magnesia and sulphate of lime. The waters are quite drinkable but some of them have a decided aperient effect on the newcomer. Bore water is not used for drinking when better water is available. Even with the solids up to several hundred grains to the gallon, the water is not hard in the technical sense, that is there is never much carbonate of lime in it, but quite to the contrary it is marvellous water to wash in, owing to the presence of the soda. We all did some washing at this bore and were astonished at the unexpected whiteness of the clothes on drying. The high soda content of the water, in addition to its high temperature, gave strong support to the theory, now abandoned, that the water was of volcanic origin. Now that the physiography and geology of the Great Artesian Basin have been thoroughly investigated, and the aquifers and intake beds are known, it is clear that the water is surface rain water that soaks into the sandstones round the rim of the basin, mainly in Queensland, and is tapped under pressure by the bores at depths from nil round the margins, where it runs out itself and makes the mound springs, to five thousand feet in the deepest bore. Still, the temperature is strangely high for such shallow depths, and the amount of soda is exceptional. High soda and carbonic acid are characteristic of the hot springs of volcanic regions.

The track from Goyder's Lagoon to Mount Gason bore lay along the slopes of the low stony tableland bordering the river flat. We could see from time to time the line of trees marking the course of the Diamantina a few miles off to the right. There were occasional sandridges that made landmarks along the track. One was called the Potato Tin. We camped near the Seven Sandhills, a curious little isolated group that I had photographed from the air years before.

Next day we came to Mt. Gason bore, another boiling stream. There was a flooded flat there too that gave us some anxious moments in crossing. The old station buildings were of good stone, but the roofs were gone and the place in ruins. Bore water had been laid on to the house and hot water could still be drawn off from a standpipe. There was a one-room building down by the track with a roof on, that was used by the passing drovers. The walls were decorated with charcoal drawings, some not without merit, and legends expressing very strong views on the character of certain drover-s, with particular reference to the rations they provided. We left another note here for the mail, in case they missed the first, saying we would wait a day or two at the Mona Downs letter-box five miles further on.

From Mt. Gason to Marree along the track, and particularly near the river in this neighbourhood, there are occasional flat-topped hills standing out in the lower ground where erosion has been more rapid, remnants of an earlier and higher surface. Mt. Gason is one such, a small and symmetrical hill 110 feet high. We passed it and found the letterbox on the track a couple of miles beyond the hill, and made camp.

Next day we all did some collecting in our various spheres.

I climbed Mt. Gason. The flat top was covered with gibbers but the rest of the hill was composed of sandstone and gypsum. Mounds of flour gypsum were scattered all about the lower ground. We dug several feet down into one but were still in gypsum.

At lunch time Nurie declared he could hear a motor truck, and sure enough the mail truck appeared in the early afternoon. He had heard it at the bore, five miles away. Simpson and Marshall were on board an empty truck. They had left all the gear behind for others to lookafter. However, they had our mail and we kept the truck waiting while we hurriedly read it and wrote a few letters for the truck to take on. Marshall had some more moving picture film and had taken some pictures at the bore and would get more along the track. I had only colour film in my camera at this stage and although the results from Goyder's Lagoon, where there was some colour, were good, the pictures were, of course, not suitable for reproduction.

Next day we took the track from the letterbox for Mona Downs. The letterbox, by the way, was an empty tea chest standing beside the track. The country was poor, stony and gypseous at the letterbox, but as soon as we got down on to the flats again there was a wonderful change. There were swamps and meadows splendidly grassed and fields of yellow daisies on the sandy patches, with cotton bush, while in the lower ground there were wide areas covered with the purple flowers of a creeping plant, a very attractive Swainsona. The lignum in the swamps was all dead, as it had been at Goyder's Lagoon, a reminder that things were not always like this.

It was eleven miles to the river. On the way we saw a group of five kangaroos, the only ones seen on the whole journey. Emu tracks were common, and there were many ibis in the swamps. It had been noticed again how clearly tracks stood out on the gibber plains we had just left. A single vehicle track is plain to see for years after it has been made, and footprints of animals last an astonishing time. A little study had just revealed the reason for this. The gibbers are only a layer of stones on top of crusty soil, and they are pressed down by the weight of the vehicle or animal. The wind blows the sand into the depressions. and fills them, burying the sunken gibbers. The sand is a lighter colour than the dark-red gibbers and the sand-filled tracks thus stand out on a darker background and are preserved almost indefinitely. The track of a vehicle becomes two lines of sand.

The track we were following led us to a crossing over the Warburton just below where the Diamantina divides into the two channels, the Warburton and Kallakoopah, The crossing was newly corduroyed with timber and vehicles had recently been over it. We could not tell the depth of water owing to its turbidity, but went boldly in and found it was only a foot or so, and the camels slipped and plunged across on the logs. There were several tracks on the other side, but the best seemed to bear to the left so we followed it. After a few miles we realized that there was something wrong. Other tracks branched off, and it appeared that they were all just odd tracks about the run. After seven miles we camped at a water hole among sandhills to Which a track led us. Some black duck that were on it flew away. There were a few cattle and a couple of horses grazing near by. These and five cattle belonging to Clifton Hills seen near Andrewilla Waterhole were the only stock we saw in the four hundred miles from Birdsville to Marree. We passed through five old stations - Goyder's Lagoon, Mt. Gason, Cowarie, Kalamurina and Poonarunna - and all were melancholy ruins except Cowarie.

After making camp I walked to a high sandhill a mile away to get a view and try to locate the homestead, but there was nothing to be seen but flats and sandridges and vegetation, with the gum-tree line of the Kallakoopah to the west. We never found any homestead. The people were newcomers and we had not been able to get any information as to where or how they were settled. We only knew their name was Oldfield, which was not much help. There were some old sticks at the top of the sandridge, which I set fire to, as it was getting dark, on the chance of attracting attention. Pulling at these I found some were fastened together, and then discovered that they were part of a timber pyramid that had fallen over and become half buried in the sand. It was Wadamoolooloo Hill, and this was the old trig. station. I hastily put the fire out. I have an admiration and respect for the memory of our old surveyors, and in any case it would be a crime to obliterate a trig station. It was rather a surprise to find that some of the trig. hills were only sandhills. Great use had been made of the flat-topped hills where there were any, but over vast areas the only elevations were sandhills.

There was a crossing over the Warburton marked on the map Bulkalara Crossing, about eight miles below our camp, and I decided to go to this and cross to the south side of the river again in case we should get cut off. The crossing was just below a long waterhole. At the crossing we found, in place of the usual steep clay banks, that there was a gentle approach to a sandy shore. The stream was rather more than fifty yards wide with running water that looked shallow. Jack took his trousers off and waded into the cold water. Like all Afghans, he was very particular about undressing in public. He found the water was little more than knee deep, with a firm bottom, but muddy on the far bank. Coming back he tried to put his trousers on standing in the water, while his feet were free of mud, but lost his balance with one leg in, and fell over and was completely soaked. I then took Snowy in and made the far bank, after a little trouble in the mud, and Jack led the string safely across on foot. The crossing made a good colour photograph, with Jack's blue shirt one of the high-lights.

We went on down the left bank of the river for seven miles and camped. A track to Cowarie was marked here on the map, but we saw only a few traces of it on the higher ground.

There were quite a few rabbits along the Warburton, in burrows under the dead lignum bushes. Feed was poor along the river. It was always best in the sandridges, more sparse and scattered in lower patches and "crab holes" on the gibber plains, least on the clay flats near the river.

In this part of its course the Warburton was a channel some fifty yards wide between steep clay banks twenty to forty feet high, with shallow running water connecting a series of deeper holes. It was obvious, on account of the water, that we could do nothing about the fossil bones, and we abandoned all thought of it.

During the day Albert took the gun and walked along the river for a time, but had no luck. We thought we had lost him for a while and had a short halt till he appeared again.

We missed Andy and his conversation round the camp, and had to rely chiefly on Albert for entertainment, and he was a fair substitute. He still had long arguments with his camel, which seemed to take little heed. Jack told him a camel could not roll on him on account of its hump, but he said his would find a hole in the ground and stick its hump into that. I asked Jack it he knew anything about djinns, and he said his father had told him that they were lights like a fire in the night and if you go to one it moves to another place.

We were now only eleven miles from Cowarie Station, which is on the Derwent, a tributary of the Warburton, and a few miles up from the junction. I took a bearing from the map, and for the first time in my life I made a mistake with compass variation, adding the easterly variation to the true bearing instead of subtracting it, with the result that I was eight degrees out in my course and when we came to the Derwent there was no sign of the station and we had to go another mile and a half upstream to find it - no great hardship, but very annoying to me. The tableland edge receded up the Derwent and our way lay across flats with many claypans full of water. We had a little difficulty at one running gutter. In the last five miles there were sandridges between the river and the flats and we travelled in these. The herbage on them was wonderful, and flowers were everywhere. It was very bright and colourful compared with the forbidding red sand and grey spinifex of the Simpson Desert. Here the sand was light yellow and covered with yellow daisies, yellow and mauve stocks, everlastings, flowering broom and the beautiful "lilac" or Swainsona, with annual saltbush and other plants. Spinifex was absolutely gone, and we never saw a single bush of it in the whole of the Lake Eyre region. This is a remarkable thing, when one considers there is nothing but dense spinifex a hundred miles to the north. It may be that it is inimical to gypsum, in which the Lake Eyre soils abound. There is no difference in climate, and all is sand.

Cowarie had been a big place. There were all the usual buildings-"Government House", men's quarters, stores, shops, stockyards - but now only an old retired drover and his wife lived there, with a young half-caste man, among these relics of former great and spacious days. They had been there three years. A niece from down south - a quiet little seventeen-year-old girl in a navy blouse and trousers tucked into her elastic-sided boots - had been staying with them but was leaving by the next mail. Old Morley said she had become a good rider. They were evidently trying to get some stock, but we saw nothing but a herd of goats. Morley told Jack he would have killed a bullock if he had known we were coming, perhaps a brave gesture, but he did kill four goats for us, two to be salted next day and two fresh, for we were out of meat and it was still over a fortnight to Marree. It was obvious that the old station could not offer hospitality now, so we went a quarter of a mile up the stream and camped and had our lunch. The Derwent was a well-defined creek with sandy bottom and lined with gum trees, but it was dry. We were told there had been a waterhole at the station twenty-five feet deep but it was now silted up and there was no hole. This is what happens under heavy stocking and erosion. However, there was a good well and windmill and we were able to get rid of our "white" water from the rivers and claypans and to fill up with clear well water. The white water never settles while you are carrying it, and it makes poor tea. No doubt it does come clear in the waterhole after standing a year or so in drought times but in wet seasons it seems to be permanently white, and clear water is only to be found on the gibber plains away from the river flats.

There was some firewood from dead box gums at our camp, and it was needed, for the weather was still very cold. Wild pigeons were nesting in the acacias by the camp. They did not fly off the nest when discovered.

Later in the afternoon we had a cup of tea and a yarn at the station. Morley said the Warburton had been running since February and would run for another month, making a total of eight months. In both the previous years, 1937 and 1938, it had run, rising rather higher, but still only a channel flood. For some years before that it had not been more than a trickle. The last big flood inundating the country was in 1933, and 1918 had been the biggest flood of recent years. Except for big floods, the Kallakoopah got no water from the Diamantina, and at present would only have local run-off in it.

Morley had a lot of interesting information about the country, and we visited the homestead again after dinner and continued our yarns. Wood was scarce, the fire small, and the room very cold, but we had some coffee and our host produced a box of excellent cigars, which, as one suspected, had been a present, a birthday present. There could have been no greater hospitality than this. Mrs. Morley said it was a cold night and would be cold camping, to which we agreed, but actually we were glad to get back to the warmth of our own camp fire and our beds.

We spent most of the next day at the station. Morley pointed out some landmarks from a sandridge near by, on which there was another old trig. station. He told of swamps to go round and sandridges to cross, arid how the river lay. There had been a track along the Warburton to the stations lower down but this would be obliterated. There were several crossings over branches and tributaries to look out for, and the going was likely to be difficult in a wet season.

There was a tragic little cemetery on the side of a sandridge near the station. The headstones were almost buried in the sand and the lead lettering stood out on the surface of the abraded marble. The sand-blast had worn away the stone but left the malleable lead almost unaffected. One could read memorials to William Alfred Thomas who died in 1892, aged 19 years; and to Eugenie Patterson in 1887, aged 24 years; and to Henry Loman in 1881 at 34 years; and one wondered under what tragic circumstances death had come so early to these young people in that remote place.

While the meat was being prepared and the canteens filled we watched Morley breaking in a black filly. His methods were very slow and gentle. He had her in the usual small circular yard with a post in the middle, a yard enclosed by ten-foot log walls, and an old grey horse in with her, She was lassooed cleverly by the half-caste and allowed to run round the yard with the old horse, the end of the rawhide rope from her neck passing round the centre post. This is the first exercise in restraint. The pair kept together, the filly on the outside, and when they stopped Morley would handle the old horse and then reach across to the filly. He was soon running his hands all over her, Later he had a bridle and bit on her, and then surcingle and even hobbles. Then in a larger yard they had her by herself, without hobbles, and put reins through the rings in the surcingle, still with the rawhide halter round her neck. All went well till they pulled the reins back over her rump. The reins seemed a little too long, for they fell away behind and down to her hocks. I do not think this was intended. As soon as it happened she went mad and bolted round and round the yard. I saw her look wildly up at the top of the rails and almost decide to try to jump. There was a gate at one end, made of the light angle-iron from a windmill frame. Suddenly this apparent opening caught her eye and she dashed straight at it, crashed into it, bent it almost double, shot over the top and landed on her head the other side. I thought her neck would be broken, but not a bit of it. She sprang up, bucked and kicked, and then galloped away over the sandridge horizon, free once more. It was an amazingly sudden change from docility to wild action. There was some hair left on the iron gate but apparently no great damage had been done to the horse. Morley was not in the least perturbed. He climbed down from the rails and said he liked to see them like that, with a bit of spirit-she would make a good horse. They let out the other yarded horses and the half-caste rode off with them to bring her in again with the mob. I have seen much rougher methods, where the first lesson is to draw the horse by the rawhide rope up to the side of the yard as opportunity offers, where it suddenly finds it can't get away and struggles madly, often damaging itself on the rails, till it gives in from exhaustion and learns that man is master. This is breaking the spirit, subjugation. By the other method it is hoped that the animal will accept control through having nothing to fear. Both schools have their following. I mention these out-of-date things as being possibly of more interest to-day than an account of how to run-in a motor·car, on the same principle as Wilkinson's photographing of the camels at Oodnadatta.

We left Cowarie in the afternoon and made across country to the river again and camped on a sandridge. The sandridges here were in groups several miles apart," each group made up of three or four ridges close together, like one great sandhill with several crests. This was only seen near Cowarie, but Colson said they were all like that at the south end of the Simpson Desert. The sand was redder again in these big ridges, and there was much live sand on the crests with steep banks on the west side.

We camped on slopes covered with flowering stocks, daisies and everlastings.

Next day we followed the Warburton round a southerly bend, sometimes on the edge of the sandridges, sometimes crossing bays where the flood plain ran back into the sandridge country. Three creek crossings were almost dry and caused little trouble. There were a number of large claypans on the flats, fast drying up, and around them and along the water courses and in swampy country were many box gums, but they were all dead. The only living trees were along the main stream itself.

We camped again on a sandridge, among huge buck-bush, and several of us made buck-bush beds. The bushes are easily detached from the ground with one sweep of the shovel underneath to cut the single tap root, and two or three big ones make a wonderful bed. From then onwards it became the usual thing, scorned by Jack but enjoyed by most of us. Jack's argument was that once you make it a habit it is hard to do without it. His principle was to stay tough and you were always comfortable. So far we had only made a few camps among buck-bush, but now the plant became universal and we never had to go back to sleeping On the hard ground. The nights were almost luxurious and the shovel was in great demand at camping time.

Another five miles next morning over sandridges that came close in to the river brought us to the old Kalamurina Station, at the apex of the southerly bend in the river. We had found Cowarie occupied, Annandale only recently deserted, Kaliduwarry in ruins, though it had never been much more than a bough shelter, Goyder's Lagoon and Mt. Gason were skeletons but as they were beside the track life still went past their fallen doors; but here was desolation indeed, isolated, silent, deathly desolation that gave verisimilitude to Gregory's term the "Dead Heart of Australia".. The homestead was roofless, but the mud-brick walls still stood, breached with irregular gaps that had been the doors and windows. In the front a single door remained, with a latch and brass knob. Instead of using one of the gaps I opened this door and went in through it, so that another foot should cross the threshold after the fifty years of silence since the station closed down. Two cart wheels lying on the ground had decayed away completely, leaving only the iron rings of the tyres and hubs, and radiating lines where the spokes had been. A small railed enclosure surrounded a large dead box-gum at the front of the house, and there was a pile of stones that had once been a rock garden. The railing was probably put up to protect a small sapling possibly planted there; now. it grotesquely ringed the base of a giant skeleton. The outbuildings appeared to have been made of wattle and daub, but all the daub had fallen away. A broken piece of cut glass, purple from long exposure to the sun's rays, took the mind back to happy times around the table in the brave days before the grim desert had destroyed the illusions of the pioneers.

The Warburton here looked remarkably like the Darling, a muddy stream fifty yards across between high banks of clay, and lined with lignum and box gum. The water appeared deep but there was no obvious flow.

Our course was then due west for thirty miles across a northerly bend in the river, and then another ten miles down the river to where it appeared on maps to enter the Lake. We followed the river for a few miles over white clay flats with dead box-gums till it bore away north, and then we entered big white sandridges again, in country like the Simpson Desert but with white sand instead of red, and with buck-bush instead of spinifex. There was no timber at all. On the river flats we had come for the first time upon areas of matted dead grass, brown and extraordinarily tough and wiry, on which the camels' feet slipped. This was on the sandridges too, and proved to be chief vegetation at that time all down the eastern side of Lake Eyre.

We camped that night in sandridge desert again at Camp 40. There were wild camels about, and some had got among our beasts while they were grazing, so Jack built a yard again. We had given up this practice since leaving Birdsville. He said a bull camel might scatter our team and cause havoc. It is not uncommon for a team on the track to be attacked in this way, and Jack was obviously very apprehensive. The bulls can terrify and even kill the timid bullocks. Sure enough, just before we turned in we heard a roaring in the darkness, and Jack dashed for his old Winchester carbine. We all turned out to search, and there dimly seen was a young bull camel in fighting mood. Jack brought it down with a first shot, and then another. We went up and found it sitting down with head erect and motionless, and not a sound but the dreadful gushing out of its life blood. I went up close with my .22 rifle to end the tragic business and fired four or five shots from the side into what I thought would be its brain, but the head never moved. It was most uncanny. I might have been firing blank cartridges. I then went behind and fired into the base of the skull, when the beast immediately collapsed and never moved again. The camel must have a very small and well-protected brain. It was a melancholy affair, but appeared to have been necessary. By next morning, owing to the green fodder, the carcase had already swollen to an enormous size. Some of the party had been talking of the camel steaks that they intended cutting from it next day, but in addition to its repulsive appearance it was found to be suffering badly from mange, and the subject was dropped.

The whole of the next day was spent in travelling across the sandridges; we crossed fifty-two at a slight angle to the perpendicular in about sixteen miles. The spacing was about the same as in the desert, but the direction about fifteen degrees nearer north, being only about ten degrees west of north. This is characteristic of the eastern side of Lake Eyre.

To-day was the last day of counting sandridges, and the last full day of sandridge crossing, for to-morrow we would be on the river again and then turning south and travelling more or less parallel to them. Since leaving Andado Bore I had covered my compass box with seven hundred and ninety-two ticks with the date for each day's tally. Between Andado Station and Birdsville we had crossed seven hundred and forty-four sandridges, and in the whole journey had negotiated no less than eight hundred and six.

This sandridge country was dotted with claypans, and we passed to the north of a very long one, Lake Koolkootinnie, which appeared to have two pools of water in it but was dry at the near end. All the smaller lakes were dry. These lakes and claypans are not connected with the river but are surrounded on all sides by sandridges. It is only local rainfall that can put any water in them. We tried to cross one about a mile in diameter, with a very gypseous powdery surface, but before we got half way across the camels began to get frightened and play up, so we took fright too and came out; it was getting very boggy.

The sand was all very gypseous and is often largely composed of gypsum crystals. This makes it much more coherent than the Simpson Desert sand, so that there were often vertical faces on the sides of ridges where wind or water had caused erosion, a thing never seen in the desert. On lower slopes there was often wind sculpturing, with pillars and castles similar to the sculpturing seen on a big sandridge near Andrewilla Waterhole, though there the coherence was due to clay and not gypsum. There were gypsum "blows" on the flats, and plates of clear gypsum lying about. Some of the ridges were up to sixty feet high, and they were invariably higher and more precipitous beside claypans. The sand instead of filling the claypans seems rather to be swept up from their surfaces to build the ridges or dunes even higher. The eastern slope of the sandridges was still, as always, the steeper, but here and at this time there was invariably a steeper bank in the live sand of the crest on the western side, due to secondary east winds. Crossing the ridges in a westerly direction was considerably more laborious than it had been going east in the desert.

Albert and his Peter were still providing the fun. That day I heard him say, "Blast you, Peter, what do you keep on eating all the time for instead of trying to go down the hill properly?" Masses of flowering stocks, everlastings, broom and lilac still covered the sandridges, with the wire grass everywhere. It was tempting for the camels to take a bite as they passed a luscious plant, but Peter had a way of stopping altogether in awkward positions on steep slopes.

We camped that night on an old east-west running fence on the edge of the sandridges about a mile from the river. The remains of two fences on Cowarie, the rabbit fences at Kaliduwarry, and this one, were the only signs of fencing in seven hundred miles.

In the morning we went up to the river bend at Poonarunna Station but did not see this ruin, if any of it remains. We were possibly a mile down stream of the station site and did not search for it. The river here was a hundred and fifty yards across and appeared to be running slowly.

We were then only about ten miles from the end of the Warburton, where a branch creek, the Kalaweerina, running south, connects it to Lake Eyre. We crossed another small bend in the river by entering the sandridges again, and then another five miles along the river brought us to the Kalaweerina Creek, where we made Camp 42 in the early afternoon at the junction of the waters.

14
LAKE EYRE

LATE were now at the north end of Lake Eyre, and the last phase of the expedition was to travel down its eastern side for a hundred miles to Marree, to see to what extent the two good seasons had quickened the very core of the Dead Heart, and to test my theory that the lake is never covered all over with water at any time, but that each river that runs a flood merely spreads its waters over a portion of the four thousand odd square miles of the lake's surface in the vicinity of its own mouth. If all the rivers from all sides ran together, which probably never happens now, they would only put a few feet of water in the lake, which would disappear in a few months under the evaporation of a hundred inches a year. I had thoroughly examined the lake all over from the air, and the southern end of the North Lake from the ground, just ten years before, at the end of a drought, and there was then no water anywhere. Now I had followed the full-flowing Diamantina down, though it was only a chan-nel flood, and the next thing was to see what became of its waters.

The Kallakoopah and the Warburton, according to the maps, form a closed ring which the Macumba, which has already been joined by the Finke, joins just north of the lake. Probably some of the waters from this ring enter the lake near the Macumba junction, but we could not reach that point, twelve miles away, as all further progress westward or northward was blocked by the waters of the Kalaweerina and Warburton, and only the south was open to us. It was obvious at any rate that the Kalaweerina was an important connection to the lake from this ring.

The country is so flat and the watercourses so ramified that it is practically impossible to distinguish them. Any of the rivers flowing back water up all parts of the ring. At our camp three waterways met - the Warburton which we had followed down, a continuation of it towards the west or a loop back of the Kallakoopah, whichever it is, and the Kalaweerina running away south. The three looked like great still canals. The Warburton was about two hundred yards across and the Kalaweerina about seventy-five yards. The waters appeared at first to be flowing northward up the Kalaweerina from the lake to the Warburton, from observation of floating sticks, but movement both ways was later noted and no definite conclusion could be arrived at. The great body of water in the Warburton seemed to be motionless. Water birds were in great numbers and varieties. There were ducks, pelicans, seagulls, terns and shags. The water was saline but drinkable. Little fish were jumping but we got no bites on the lines. Rabbits were more plentiful here than anywhere along the river, but they were not numerous; they were just starting to breed up again. Trees had practically disappeared from river banks. There were only a few acacias at the camp, and an occasional stunted box. The dominant plant was masses of buck-bush. Since we entered the Lake Eyre sandridges a new bird had appeared in considerable numbers, the orange-fronted chat, a beautiful bird with jet black throat, orange on the underparts and yellow back.

We all had a bath and shave at this camp. It was too cold to enjoy bathing. Albert surprised us all by jumping in fully clothed and splashing about. He said he wanted to wash his clothes at the same time. One could not wade across the Kalaweerina and it seemed too cold to swim over. I made a small raft next morning with empty water canteens and paddled across. A pair of canteens made a crazy affair that was too unstable and only floated satisfactorily upside down, so I had to sit on the submerged decking and carry my clothes. There was nothing further to be seen in a short walk on the other side, and I returned with only a large bouquet of yellow daisies that were growing more luxuriantly there.

The east side of Lake Eyre has never been accurately mapped. The trigonometrical survey had not been carried down that side. The present-day maps are based on J. W. Lewis's route sketches made on his exploration of 1874-5, with some additions. Where modifications are made to features along Lewis's tracks the newer versions are less correct. The same applies to Winnecke's maps of the upper Hay River and the Tarlton Range area. Where the sketches of these old surveyors are departed from, the maps have suffered. I would have been saved some trouble if I had had Lewis's original maps with me on this journey. There are many arms stretching out eastward from the lake, and in addition numerous scattered lakes, large and small, some up to ten or twenty miles long, not connected to the main lake at all. These lakes and arms would be sure to be boggy if not under water, and we were obviously going to have some problems in getting round them without being cut off and having to retrace our steps. It would be impossible to distinguish an arm of the lake from a separate lake. The country is as bad as any in the Simpson Desert, and has never been occupied at all. Detailed mapping would be a long and arduous task, and has not so far been justified. We found difficulty as we progressed in reconciling our position with features on the map, as all lakes were not marked and those that were gave only an approximate shape and position. We wanted to keep as close to the lake as possible and to visit its shores at least two or three times.

We started off by following the Kalaweerina Creek down for eight miles. It opened out to two hundred and fifty yards wide, and became a wonderful sheet of water with pelicans, swans, geese, ducks, gulls and terns on it. The water was deep and blue, no longer white, for the mineral salts cause flocculation and rapid settlement of the colloidal clay. At one time we were puzzled by what seemed to be low moving clouds, constantly changing and appearing and disappearing. This proved to be clouds of birds on the wing in the light of the setting sun, the light catching them differently as they changed their direction. It was obvious abundantly true that aboriginals would come to the lake for birds' eggs, an argument used in favour of the permanency of the water, but I was convinced that this great congregation of birds was entirely temporary and seasonal, for I had seen the lake utterly deserted.

At the end of eight miles the Kalaweerina Creek opened out into a wide arm that ran away east and cut us off from further progress south. The map shows the creek continuing on past the end of this arm for another five miles and then entering Lake Eyre proper, and the arm turning south-east and entering the lake some twelve miles further down. Whether the arm that cut us off from the lake should be considered a branch of the creek or an arm of the lake it is difficult to say. Like other marginal swamps it might be considered as either. If we were unable to visit the real shores of the lake here we would have to go a long way down the side before we had another opportunity, owing to the ramification of arms or branches. The water was only a few inches deep in the arm, and the distance across about half a mile, but it was too great a risk for the camels, and we were obliged to camp on the shore. If we had got over we should probably have had to come back the same way as we would have been going on to a sort of island.

138

We were now in lake country proper. It was a most desolate camp on the gypsum slopes that formed the shore of the arm. There was no vegetation at all near the shores, owing to the salt and gypsum, no timber anywhere in sight, and a cold west wind was blowing. The outlook over the perfect flatness of the inhospitable shores and the limitless sheet of shallow water was bleak and depressing. The only wood was a few dillon bush or nitre bush, a wretched looking plant with very tough and brambly limbs, difficult to collect and unsatisfactory for fire-building even when it has been battered into more or less tractable pieces. We made a fireplace by digging into the gypsum bank, to get the most out of our small supply of wood. Later in the evening the wind died down, the little fire burned brightly, the full moon shone over the still water and the prospect lost some of its harshness under the gentle influence of night. The straight line of the shore divided the level earth into two halves, the shining water and the bare dull ground, and these two, with the moon above, the pinpoint of the fire and the silence, comprised all the simple elements that made up the strange stark scene.

By this time not one of the camels was free from mange, and some of them were in a bad way with it, so that though the loads were light we were slowing up. The camels required urging just when we were most impatient to get on.

Next day we followed down the arm of the lake in a south-south-east direction. After about eight miles the water came to an end and the bed was dry. We saw no more birds leaving the creek; the water was probably too salty for them. The branch then turned eastward and we were compelled to follow it, as the surface was too boggy to attempt to cross. We caught a glimpse of the main lake from the top of a sandridge at this point and it appeared to be dry, but our course was taking us further and further away from it, and it was camping time before the eastern end of the arm was reached. Buck-bush was still abundant, with plenty of flowering plants and vegetation on the sandridges and everywhere except along the saline shores. Everyone but Jack and Albert was now making buck-bush beds. I observed for latitude that night to check our position.

On the following morning we continued in an easterly direction for another five or six miles to round the end of the arm. It had several spurs in it and we had to go round all these branch arms, thus losing a lot of time.

Owing to the sandridges we could never see the bays till we came right upon them, after rounding each one we would turn hopefully southward only to be forced back again to round the next. Eventually we came to a narrow neck. I led Snowy across this. Sand was encroaching from the far side and though moist, the ground was firm, and the string safely followed. At last we were going south once more, but by this time were a good twelve miles or so from the lake. There was another arm shown on the map sixteen miles to the south so I decided to go down to this before trying to turn in to the lake again. After half an hour's travelling another lake surface suddenly appeared in front and to the east of us, and it looked as if we might be on an island. I was inclined to turn back at once, but decided to investigate a little further before doing so. We went south-west and eventually rounded what proved to be a bay and then found ourselves in lake-free sandhills, and all was well. It was seen that the arm we had just crossed had followed us round. I discovered later that Lewis had crossed at this very place, but we did not have his original route sketch with us as I wrongly supposed that later maps would be more correct. Another ten miles to the south brought us to the shores of the next arm, a very wide bay in the lakeside.

The shores of this bay were most desolate. Barren gypsum slopes led up to the sandridges behind, and a bitter cold wind was blowing dust off the lake surface. There was no fuel. We turned back into the sandridges to camp and found a few dead trees in a hollow, so we made a fire, and all hands turned to and built a wind-break of buck-bush in black-fellow fashion half-way round it, a suggestion of Jack's that proved most effective. After we had finished our dinner of braised goat and green peas, followed by stewed apricots and blancmange, the wind died down, the moon shone brightly, and this most dead and desolate place in the world gradually grew quite friendly as a sense of well-being infused us under the influence of warmth, food, rest and the wafting fragrance of the tobacco smoke. It had been a long and tiring day. We were making earlier starts now and travelling not less than eight hours a day.

The map indicated that this bay had a smooth and rounded contour but again we found this was far from being the case. We started off eastward to round its end but were immediately confronted with an arm lying across our path. Crocker and Fletcher walked across this one, and said it was too boggy for camels, so we had to go round it. At last we were able to

Exacting directions.

Fletcher with a womma.

turn south along the broad end of the bay. After four miles another arm suddenly shot out in a south-easterly direction and again barred our way south. We made rather a long lunch halt here. There was an island in a bay in this arm about half a mile from the shore, and I rather disgusted Fletcher by saying that the scene reminded me of Sydney Harbour, except that one had heard there was a bridge there. Actually there was a resemblance, for the sandridges were covered with the dark wire-grass which made them look quite black in the distance, as if covered with trees. The white dry bed of the arm with its islands and the dark indented shore line with capes and bays gave exactly the appearance of a great sheet of water enclosed by wooded hills. The vertical scale was very deceptive. When the grass looked like trees the points rose up to mountain spurs instead of fifty foot sandridges.

Everywhere the sandridges ended abruptly and steeply on the south shores of lakes, but the northern shores rose gently from the margins over hard gypseous slopes into the sand ridges beyond. This is due to the prevailing winds being southerly and causing a general northerly movement of the sand along the direction of the ridges.

We dug a three-foot hole in the lake bed a hundred yards from the shore. The first two feet was through gypseous sand below which was sandy clay saturated with salt water.

The camels had to go round this small bay but Crocker and Fletcher walked across to the island and on to the far side, saying afterwards that the going was firm and we might have taken the team across. The main arm then ran away south-east for four miles. Half way along it there appeared to be a patch of water in the middle.

This arm proved to be the last obstacle for the time being, for after rounding it we were able to make south again for Cooper Creek, which, according to the maps, entered a still more southerly arm of the same bay. After about four miles through gently-rolling sandridges, we came to a broad valley or depression crossing them, about a mile wide, and at the bottom of it we found a narrow winding lane of sand of a texture rather coarser than that of the sandridges. There was not a tree or a shrub along this watercourse; the whole valley was bare except for the ephemeral grasses. So this was the end of the famous Cooper Creek, the mighty river that has its origin eight hundred miles away in the Great Dividing Range of Queensland, whose floods carry both life and des¬truction half way across an arid continent! The sandy bed was too narrow and too shallow to take any considerable quantity of flood water, even as much as the channel flood we had just seen in the Diamantina, and there were no signs of rises or lateral spreading, yet the clear, coarse nature of the sand and the absence of vegetation in the bed indicated that water does still run here occasionally, though it would be mainly local drainage and not Queensland floods. The last flood that reached the Birdsville track was in 1917, but there is no evidence that it got as far as the lake, though this is probable. No one attempts to visit the lake in times of flood.

We crossed the valley and began the usual search for firewood before making camp. In the sand ridges beyond we found some scattered needlebush, some of it actually living, and camped among it. Crows were nesting in the trees and there were eggs in the nests. Albert was going to cut down one tree with a nest in it - they were only brambly affairs about twelve feet high-but Jack told him not to on the grounds that it was the poor b---'s home. Jack's reactions in cases like this were often unexpected. Like the Arabs, he seemed to have a dual personality which made him capable of either great cruelty or surprising kindness. These people's feelings, their loves and hates, their rewards and punishments, seem to run to much greater extremes than ours, particularly when translated into actions; we say "I could kill him for that", but leave it at words. Jack once told us how he tied up a camel that bit him and bashed out several of its teeth with an axe - it was Punjab, the camel that Marshall rode-and another time he said with conviction that he would kill the man who had left a bogged camel to die at Goyder's Lagoon.

According to the map, this crows' nest camp should have been about fifteen miles at least from the lake, for there was no sign of the long north-west trending arm shown on the map with the Cooper running into the near end of it. We started off westward for the lake margin next morning, across the low rolling sandridges. Although Lewis had marked the area with "high sandridges" one could not agree with him. By our standards they were no more than sandy undulations rising perhaps thirty or forty feet above the valleys. For a few miles nothing was to be seen but sandridges. Then a narrow lake appeared to the south, coming up from the south-east. At five miles we were at the north end of this lake. There was shallow water in it over a distance of about a mile, varying in width from twenty to a

144

hundred yards, and two inches deep where we examined it. It was brine, with a salt crust an inch thick all round the edge. As with all lakes in the sandridges, the water was from local rainfall. There are no drainage lines and no obvious catchments except the lake floors themselves, which are simply wind-swept flats surrounded by sandhills. No birds come near these very salty waters, which most of the time are saturated solutions of salt.

After another mile and a half we topped a sandridge, and there suddenly before us lay Lake Eyre stretching in a dead white plain to the western horizon. It was all the more dramatic as we did not expect to see it for at least another two hours, though by this time it was obvious that the mapping in this region has been very sketchy. From the top of the sandridge along the shore there was no sign of water as far as the visible· horizon some six miles away, so Fletcher, Crocker and I at once started to walk out on the lake. The surface was of damp buff-coloured gypseous clay in which our feet sank about half an inch. It would be typical bull-dust in dry weather. This continued unchanged for the two and a half miles of our walk. We sank several two-foot holes on the way out, disclosing nothing but clayey sand saturated with brine. There were odd sticks of wood lying about, and we found a log big enough for all three to sit on at the end of the walk. This is driftwood, and shows that there has been at some time a considerable flow of water on the lake. I had seen driftwood in the south-eastern corner of the lake on my former visit, and there is no doubt that the wood was brought in by the Frome River entering at that corner. The Frome rises in the Northern. Flinders Ranges, in sparsely timbered country, and is a comparatively short and swift stream. Heavy rains in the Flinders cause the Frome to flood at least once every few years, and the waters, carrying considerable debris, can easily reach the lake, but it is questionable whether normal Frome floods could carry timber half way up the lake side and leave it so close in-shore. By every piece of timber lying on the lake there was a hole scooped out by wind eddies, and these holes had recently held water from local rainfall but were now dried up. Round their margins there was a black band half an inch wide, which closer inspection showed was made up of the dead remains of many kinds of insects, among which ladybirds, beetles, and grasshoppers were most conspicuous. They must have blown out over the surface from the shore till stopped by the water in the pools. Ants were frequently seen all the way out, the entrances to their holes protected by mounds of clay, little columns with a narrow waist like cotton reels stood up on end. Spiders' webs were fairly common on the surface too. The spiders lived in holes in the crust beside their webs. Two species were collected and they both proved to be new to science. The presence of these creatures so comparatively far from the shore shows that normally there is no water on the lake near the shores for long periods. My previous study of the south-eastern part of the lake had shown that although the surface looks level, there is an imperceptible fall between the shores and the level salt crust in the area I have called the bull-dust margin, which is up to four miles wide in the south. Lewis found a fall of two and a half feet in seven miles at the north end. The salt was seventeen inches thick at a distance of twelve miles from the south end of the North Lake when I was there ten years before. We did not go out as far as the salt crust on this occasion. The place was at about the middle of the eastern side of the North Lake, near to and south of the Cooper entrance, though we did not actually see what became of the Cooper. We had left it as a well-defined water-course running a little north of west only eight miles behind us, but the maps show it going rather indefinitely north-west into an arm of the lake and eventually reaching the lake some sixteen miles north of where we were. The Cooper in rare floods like the 1917 one might bring down timber such as we saw there and deposit it on the marginal zone of the lake. Whenever it was that the wood was washed in, it was long enough ago for the ants and spiders to be able to colonize the first two or three miles of the lake margin.

We could not follow the shores down on account of another long arm to the south of us that ran out in a south-easterly direction. We decided to go round this arm and then go due south till we met the shore of the lake again near the south end. We camped that night a few miles down the arm. It was the coldest night of the whole journey, the minimum thermometer recording 22.8°F. "at grass", which was where we slept. The days were dull, with bleak winds, but the temperature rose to sixty degrees or so during the day. The highest recorded day temperature was seventy-eight degrees near Charlotte Waters, and generally the daily maximum was between sixty and seventy degrees.

We saw another copper-coloured snake during the day, but failed to catch it.

Next day we found it was a further eight miles before we reached the end of the arm we were camped on. Near the end of it there was some slushy salt or "near" water. We crossed the end of the arm and found the sandridges on the south side of it were seventy feet by aneroid above the lake floor. We now went due south, crossing the white sandridges at a small angle. In the lake country it is only on the edges of lakes or claypans that the sandridges have sharp crests with live sand. Most of the country is gently-rolling, with sandridges like the broad ocean swells that only steepen up as the shoal water of the coast is reached. There is a remarkable similarity in this respect between desert and ocean, though in this desert. the "ocean" is at a higher level, and the "land" - that is, the lake floors - at a lower level. There were numerous claypan islands scattered through this sand sea we were in. Some of them were quite small, less than a mile in diameter. They were like holes scooped out of the sand, with the sandridges higher on their southern and western sides. The remarkable thing is that they persist. One would think that the sand would encroach on them and fill them. It must be that the depressions form air eddies that keep the floors swept clean. They were quite hidden, unless very big, till one arrived at the very edge and looked down on them as into a crater. The smaller clay-pans in the Simpson Desert were of the same type.

The only timber in the country was occasional needle bush, some of it living, and even rarer acacia which was mostly dead. It was difficult to find firewood. The whole country was covered with the dead wiry grass in brown mats and tufts, looking black in the distance like heath on moorland.

The camels' feet slipped on it, slowing up our pace. The crests of the sandridges were still decorated with flowers and buck-bush, particularly where there was fresh live sand, but now it was beginning to dry off. The pretty orange-fronted chats were about in small numbers, and an occasional skylark had been noted ever since we came into the lake country. The herbage and the few birds mitigated the usual awful desolation of this region. It is hard to believe that in a few months all the vegetation can die and actually blow away, but I had seen it absolutely bare except for the butts of a few dead bushes. Ten years before it had been very difficult from the air to determine the shores of the lake, the whole country looking a uniform pink colour. Now the dark sandridges clothed with vegetation would stand out in strong contrast to the white lake surface. Times such as these come perhaps once in ten years. As I rode across the sandridges in the cold wind I noticed small plants, dead and already blown over, anchored loosely by a few remaining roots, and des¬ribing little circles in the sand. Soon they would lose their hold and blow away. Here in this vast, depressing and long-dead region the Psalmist's simile was starkly clear: "The days of man are but as grass, for he flourisheth as a flower of the field. For as soon as the wind goeth over it, it. is gone, and the place thereof shall know it no more."

Towards the end of the day we saw a lake close to the west of our course and went over to it. It was about three miles long and a mile and a half wide. As it curved away south-east we decided to cross it near the, top end where it was about three quarters of a mile wide. I walked ahead leading Snowy, and the riding camels and the string silently followed. It was rather a risky experiment, and I could feel the silence behind me. The surface was the usual damp gypseous clay, with no water, identical with the margins of the main lake. The camels' feet sank in, but nothing like as deeply as they had at Goyder's Lagoon. At three parts of the way over Jack began to talk and joke, and soon everyone joined in. The tension was relieved, and the bogey of the bottomless mud was temporarily laid. Just before the far side was reached it became rather worse but we made the shore safely. Actually the mud is practically bottomless on the main lake, but the gypsum crystals in the upper layers give it some stability. Once the surface breaks through it is very dangerous for camels. Their long legs may go right down and it is almost impossible for them to extricate themselves; in fact it is a very difficult proposition to get them out at all and might take a day's digging and hauling. This makes camel travelling in flooded country after rain a trying business and to be avoided. Quite a lot of our journey since leaving the Mulligan had been in this sort of country, but so far we had avoided the worst places and good fortune had supported our care.

The rise to the top of the sandridge on the west side from the floor of this lake was sixty-five feet. From its crest we could see Lake Eyre three miles away to the west, a wide white sweep to the horizon, and what was much more attractive, away off forty or more miles to the south-east stood a flat-topped hill. The depressing effect of the desert was shown up by the spontaneous rise in everyone's spirits at the sight of this distant hill.

The sandridge by the lake was as usual well covered with flowering stocks and buck-bush, and a little beyond there were the requisite few dead acacias for firewood, so we made camp, after eight and half hours of steady going. We lost sight of our hill at the camp and never saw it again. The low lake bed that we were looking over, assisted perhaps by mirage, may have made the long view from the top of the sandridge possible.

The objective now was to reach the neck connecting the lake that receives the waters of the Frome and Clayton Rivers with Lake Eyre North. This lake deserves a separate name and I will refer to it as Clayton Lake as there is already a Lake Frome east of the Flinders Ranges, not associated in any way with the Frome River. This neck is in the south-eastern corner of Lake Eyre North and the Clayton Lake comes up to it from the south-east. A few miles to the west is the narrow channel connecting Lake Eyre North with Lake Eyre South, which latter stretches away to the south-west. This corner of the lake had been the scene of my investigations. on the ground in 1929 and I was very anxious to revisit the spot to see if there had been any changes or signs of flooding in the past ten years, for previously there had been no water anywhere and we had taken a motor truck out as far as the salt crust and then followed the crust round the lake for twenty miles. Only some mud between the salt crust and the bull-dust margin had prevented us from getting on to the salt and motoring to the centre of the lake. To visit this place it was necessary to cross the Clayton neck, and this would also open a direct route to Marree up the Frome River past the old Muloorina Station, the way I had brought the truck out ten years before. If we were unable to cross the neck it was another two day's journey round the Clayton Lake, with possibly some difficulty in crossing the Clayton which had been running and would be boggy.

Our course was now south till we should meet the edge of Lake Eyre North, and then along the shore to the neck. This course should take us past the end of a very large horse-shoe lake marked on the maps, but we saw no signs of it at all. The general level fell as we neared the lake margin, which we were approaching at an acute angle. Finally we came to the shore. The shore line was here very straight, with a low ridge some fifteen feet high running along it, a coastal dune, and behind, low parallel ridges in moor-like country. There were no high sandridges near the lake at this end. No water was visible.

In less than three miles along the shore we came to the neck of the Frome - Clayton entrance. This was some five miles sooner than expected, and indicated that the lake at the previous night's camp had been one already marked on the map, and that we had on the day before crossed the map position of the great horseshoe lake shown surrounding the north end of the camp lake and stretching eight miles wide across our path. This horseshoe lake is either non-existent or badly out of position.

Our route surveying was not carried out as carefully as usual in the lake region owing to the country being already mapped, and when it was found that the mapping was very sketchy it was rather too late to do more. We found the features were in general as marked on the maps, but several arms extended further east than indicated, and we would place the shore of the lake south of the Cooper entrance as much as eight miles to the east of its marked position, eliminating the bulge in the middle of the east side.

We arrived at the neck at mid-day, and after some lunch we made a preliminary examination. It was a little over a mile across, with some slushy gypsum in the middle, and was quite safe for men on foot, but camels were another matter. The wet part looked like coarse sand but closer inspection showed the sand to be gypsum crystals. We decided to try to cross at once. I wanted Jack to divide the string into two halves, as the long line churns up the mud, but he was against this. I walked in, leading Snowy, and the string followed. A hundred yards, two hundred yards, half a mile, and then we were on the part with a wet surface. Half way over and the far shore began to seem quite near. It looked as if we were going to make it. Then suddenly a camel went down to the belly-poor old Grundy, who had the big boxes and the heaviest load. We all stopped, and the camels stood trembling with fear. I thought they might stampede, but they seemed frozen to the spot. Jack and Nurie quickly took the load and saddle off, while we stood by wondering when another camel would go down. Old Grundy, who seemed to know the drill, rolled over and extricated himself, to my surprise. His load was soon on again, the string turned tail and made back to the shore. It was a relief to see them arrive safely. It was not worth further risk for a day's saving of time.

I decided to walk on with Crocker and Fletcher, and left Jack to take the camels back, with instructions to make camp wherever he could find some firewood, but not more than a mile from the shore, and to light a fire on a sandridge after dark, as I expected it would be long after sunset before we got back.

We found that the strip of water in the neck was about a quarter of a mile wide and never more than half an inch deep, while the rest of the surface was gypseous silt tessellated with small cracks, a feature of all claypan floors. There was a thin salt crust where the water had evaporated. Six inches below the surface the clay was full of the typical flat gypsum crystals, rather larger than a penny, Our footprints were scarcely more than heel marks, but it was just a little too treacherous for the camels.

It was over six miles along the southern shores of the North Lake to the channel connecting to the South Lake, and we did not reach it till sunset, at a point some half mile south of the North Lake end, but still north of the place where I had examined it before. The channel is nowhere more than a few hundred yards wide. At the old spot it had shown just the same flat white crusty surface as any part of the lake margin or its numerous arms, but here it did not look like the lake floor at all. There were gutters in the bed, running crosswise and lined with shrubs, that had clearly taken the run-off from rainfall on the immediate shores. This was something quite new, to find vegetation on the floor of any lake or claypan in this region. It showed that the soil was sweet and proved that the brines of the lakes can never pass through the channel now. The inwash from the shores and the presence of the plants clearly indicated that the channel was on the way to obliteration at its north end.

It was too late to search for the old place to look for signs of the holes with their little spoil-heaps beside them that we had made with the post-hole borer, but it was obvious here that water had not passed along the channel in either direction for a very long time, or these little cross water-courses with their vegetation would not be there, but rather salt and gypsum, with signs of scour or driftwood. It was quite unlike the Clayton neck. The south end of the South Lake is often covered with water that can be seen from the railway and runs in from Stuart's Creek and numerous other short creeks from the south, but I have always held that this water does not extend up into the North Lake.

Half a mile from the mouth of the channel was the point where we had entered the lake with our truck. We found the place just before dark and to my astonishment there were the tracks of the truck leading out into the lake, almost as clear as the day we left them ten years before! We followed them out till they turned west a mile and a half from the shore. There was just enough light remaining to photograph them at a point where we had been bogged and subsequently gone round the bog, making a loop off the original track.

By this time it was almost dark and we were far out on the lake. I took a compass bearing across a bay to the point five miles away that marked the Frome entrance, and we began the long walk over the lake in a direct line for it. It was soon pitch dark, but a star was rising over our point to guide us. It was a question whether it was easier to walk all the way on the level crusty surface of the lake or to make in to the shore and then along the uneven sandridges with their tufts of grass. The latter would have been very rough going in the dark so we chose the former.

Lake Eyre is eerie enough by day; in total darkness it is a hundred times more so. We could not see the shore. The only things visible except the stars and ourselves were occasional emu tracks on the surface at our feet. The depressions had become filled with salt and stood out white like chalk marks on a grey slate. We might have been in the middle of this dead lake with its unfathomable mud beneath the thin crust under our feet. I had actually camped and slept on the lake, but it was all a new experience to my companions. I felt confident that there would be no change in the surface, but the others may have dreaded what the next step might bring forth. Nevertheless, it was even for me a weird ex-perience, and I was by this time very tired. The distance seemed interminable as we dragged our weary feet over the soft surface. At last, after nearly two hours, we found ourselves walking up the slopes of the shore and into the sandridges again; then over the narrow point, and there across the neck was the bright beacon of Jack's fire, hidden till then by the point. It was still over a mile away, but after a rest on the shore we started the half hour's tramp through the slush across the neck, and at last threw ourselves down by the fire. I at least was thoroughly exhausted. The camp was only a quarter of a mile away. I asked Jack what sort of dinner there was and he answered with unexpected enthusiasm, "Bloody good!" We went on to the camp, but it was some time before I felt like tackling the dinner. When I did I realized that it was something out of the box, even for Albert. He had made the most of a free afternoon, and it was a suitable occasion, for not only was it our last night on the shores of the lake; but it proved to be the last dinner but one that Albert would cook for us. He had done a wonderful job right through, and his industry and enthusiasm never waned. That night he put on for us a three course meal, consisting of pea soup and the last of the canned meat, with boiled onions and potatoes, followed by a strawberry blancmange, the whole accompanied by large quantities of cocoa. Such a meal was never before prepared on the shores of Lake Eyre, nor after it is there likely to be any such. It completely immobilized me. I fell into my sleeping bag and knew no more till dawn. There was no question of buck-bush that night.

Next morning we turned our backs on Lake Eyre and went south-east along the shores of Clayton Lake with the object of crossing the Clayton at the first opportunity. There was a track marked on the maps from the Cooper to Muloorina Station, crossing the Clayton near the lake; we thought we might find this track, but in any case decided to make from wherever we crossed direct to Muloorina, which Jack said was now reoccupied. There was a chance we might get a lift in to Marree by truck over the last thirty miles and thus save a day. It was Sunday, August 6th, and we wanted to catch the weekly train at Marree on the Wednesday.

We made twenty miles that day along the north side of this arm of Lake Eyre, which I have called Clayton Lake, and camped at its end, where there was an island enclosed between branches of the Clayton. We had seen no water in the lake all day but it was too damp and too wide to attempt a crossing, and at the end the channels were definitely muddy. We had to pass round several arms, and crossed the neck of one which saved many miles; it was slightly boggy but was safely negotiated. We crossed another of the arms higher up, instead of rounding it, and found the going quite good. It was a cold and dreary day, but "the girls were on the towrope", and we made good progress in spite of the slippery grass.

Notwithstanding the flowers and the grasses, and occasional small birds, the Lake Eyre region had still cast its queer spell over us. All who have travelled there have felt this haunting sense of desolation and death. The song dies on the drover's lips; silence falls on the exploring party. It is like entering a vast tomb; one hesitates to break the silence. The rivers are dead, the trees are dead, but overshadowing all in the qualities of death is the very heart of the region, the great lake itself, a horrible travesty, a vast white prostrate ghost of a lake. Here times seems to have stood still for ages, and all is dead. We had seen one sluggish vein quickend in the north, the Warburton. Sea and river birds had gathered there, bringing a show of life that threw into greater relief the deadness of the rest, but the Dead Heart, the focus of a drainage basin of four hundred and fifty thousand square miles of country, will never throb again.

On that last day as I walked along leading my camel - we walked a good deal in order to keep warm - a bird, one of the orange chats, flew out of a low bush at my feet. I parted the foliage and at once three gaping little mouths stretched up from a nest. I passed on, but looked back, knowing that Jack, who followed me, never missed anything. He peered in and then looked thoughtfully at me and said, "Something living!" He too felt how strange it was that any life should begin in this sepulchre.

R. L. Crocker with a wild turkey, Hay River.

15
TOMORROW TO FRESH WOODS

THAT night's camp, No. 50, was our last in the lonely sandy wastes. Next morning we crossed some muddy claypans and then came on the Clayton River, at first an inconspicuous muddy channel on the plains. We followed this along, making one or two efforts to cross, but Snowy got into difficulties and we did not attempt it with the string. In five miles the country began to rise arid the river occupied a valley between well-defined and even stony banks. We saw an old stockyard and signs of a track; the crossing here was gravelly and safe. We could not follow the tracks beyond the crossing but once over we set a course for Muloorina Station fifteen miles away, over broadly undulating sandy country. At last the line of trees along the Frome came in sight, and then the station roofs. We found that the old station, which had been closed for over ten years and was last used as a govern¬ment camel depot till the remainder of the unwanted camels were destroyed, was now once more a hive of industry. It had been reopened as a sheep station and shearing was in full swing. The gloom of the Dead Heart vanished like a dream in this atmosphere of life and activity. We put the camels down near the shearing shed and went across to it. Well-dressed women were just taking a dainty tea, with teacups and cakes, into the shed. They asked me if I was looking for work, and seemed rather disappointed when I said I wasn't. When our identity was satisfactorily established we were treated with all the traditional hospitality of ranches the world over.

Mr. Stan. Price, who had taken up the lease, was an enterprising businessman from Peterborough, a boring contractor with a wide knowledge of the outback. He had come in at the height of a run of good seasons, and there was feed for countless sheep. How long would this last? Would the venture be a success, or had Lake Eyre lured another man to his destruction?

Some of us dined at the station that night, but we all slept in a little creek nearby and got our own breakfast in the morning at Camp 51, the last camp of the expedition. Mr. Price found it convenient to go into Marree, and could take Crocker, Fletcher and myself in the car. Albert decided to stay with

Jack and Nurie and the camels. We got them away to an early start. They would have one more night on the track before reaching Marree next morning.

Although there were good wells at Muloorina, I found they were carting water from Lake Letty bore ten miles away. I asked about this and was surprised to find that they thought so highly of the clothes-washing properties of the bore water that they went to all this trouble to get it, a quality we thought we had discovered at Goyder's Lagoon.

We left Muloorina by car later in the morning and called at Lake Letty, where we found a rebuilt homestead and the beginnings of another brave attempt to do battle with the desert.

We were now travelling in a motor car along a road. In a few hours we would be in a hotel in a town on the railway. It is true it was a very old car, and a dirt track, but we were back again in the ways of civilization; its familiar cloak seemed suddenly to enclose us as the tattered garments of the desert life fell rapidly away. Then we overtook the camels poking slowly and silently along, with Jack at the head of his team again. How well and faithfully they had served us where no vehicle could go! Now they seemed weary and shabby, out-moded and desperately slow. We would be in Marree in an hour. They might be there by noon next day. I felt mean to dash on and leave them behind, and glad that Albert had stayed. Perhaps Jack's way of life was best. I saw he felt this moment too. It was our real parting. We merely looked and waved. The expedition was over.

As soon as we reached Marree I called on old Bejah Dervish and his wife and told them that Jack would be there next day. We collected our luggage that had been sent down from Abminga and were soon dressed for ordinary life again.

The camel team arrived late next morning in the Afghan quarters, and we had the afternoon to arrange for the disposal of the equipment; scientific instruments and collections for Adelaide, camel saddles for Alice Springs, water canteens to be left for local sale, surplus stores to the Afghans. The train left that night, and we arrived back in Adelaide next day, August 10th.

And so ended the field work of the Simpson Desert Expedition.

It had provided plenty of material for work in the laboratory, and a start was made at once to arrange for the preparation and publication of the results, upon which the real lasting value of the expedition depended. The natural history collections, both botanical and biological, were sorted and sent to specialists in the various groups for identification and description; the mapping work was checked and plotted; the photographic results were examined and classified and the film edited and titled. Mr. Simpson lived to see the film but passed away a few weeks after our return.

The desert crossing had been a happy and successful adventure, arid it only needed the completion of the scientific work to bring it all to a satisfactory conclusion. But the war clouds were about to break, and before long we found ourselves engaged in the much grimmer adventure of war, which soon claimed most of us, some in the more heroic field of active service and others in training, administration or munitions. The scientific work was greatly hampered for want of workers; even its value or necessity seemed open to question. It is only now, six years after our return, when manpower has been reshuffled and adjustment to war conditions has become more stabilized, that it is again possible to pick up the threads and to make some further progress with writing and publication.

As I bring this story to a close, light is beginning to break in the darkness. The prospect of an end to this return to savagery in dimly seen, and one takes heart to look forward with hope to a chastened and readjusted world wherein right and justice rule, where all men can work in peace and goodwill for the benefit of humanity and not its destruction, and where once again one will be free to take pleasure and pride in such things as the study of deserts.

APPENDIX A

NOTES ON THE SCIENTIFIC RESULTS OF THE EXPEDITION

REPORTS by various authors on the scientific results will be appearing by the time this popular narrative is published. The Royal Society of South Australia has generously undertaken to publish them serially as they are prepared. Papers on various biological sections, and on the mineralogy of the sands, are already awaiting publication.

The chief geographical study is the source of the sand and the processes by which it has been swept up into such a remarkable series of long, straight and parallel ridges. Is the process still going on and the sandridge deserts extending, is it static, or are the desert areas receding? These problems are now being studied.

The botanical collecting was very thorough and complete. After the good seasons the time was most opportune for it, with every plant flourishing and most in flower or fruit. The botanical results should be a very satisfactory section of our contributions to natural science.

The field of biology is a much wider one, and anything approaching completeness in biological collecting requires more time than was available, and what is even more essential, a specialist in each section, who knows how and where to search, has a knowledge of the common forms and can appreciate what is rare or unique. Unfortunately we had no biologists expert in any particular direction, and 'so had collected without system everything we could lay our hands on. An ornithologist, for instance, could have kept a record of birds without necessarily bringing back a specimen of each. Bird collecting and preserving is itself a full-time job for one man. It was the most neglected of the biological sections on our journey. We took specimens of five different species of wrens and chats from the middle of the desert, beautiful little birds, but none of them new or undescribed. We made no attempt to cope with the prolific bird life of the Diamantina.

The mammals were restricted to the dingo and the mice and rats. Besides the introduced mice found round the borders of the desert, we succeeded in collecting only two forms, in spite of much digging, a fat-tailed marsupial mouse and the fawn jerboa mouse. The latter was first collected by Sturt in 1854, a pretty little hopping fellow with a brushy tail. Either the rarer small marsupials were absent or we missed them.

The insect collection was much more extensive. Some eighty different species were obtained, some of which may prove to be new to science, and one (*Vamia perloides*) is only known by a single specimen housed in the British Museum.

A hundred and five spiders were collected, representing fourteen families and twenty-eight species. Fourteen of these species were new.

The reptiles were described by the Director of the Australian Museum as an excellent collection. A few snakes were caught, and a large number of lizards of many different kinds. The lizards are much the commonest and most conspicuous inhabitants of the desert, the outstanding features of which at a glance are sand, spinifex, and lizards, in that order. Anything further has to be sought for, but a careful search reveals an astonishing number of less obstrusive plant and animal forms.

APPENDIX B

THE SUPPOSED DETERIORATION OF THE LAKE EYRE COUNTRY

FROM time to time statements are made to the effect that the seasons In the Lake Eyre country are not as good as they were, and that the country has gone back through the decrease of rainfall, through over¬stocking, through rabbits, through sand drift and erosion, through any or all of these causes, but chiefly through deterioration in rainfall. The supposed failure of the rainfall is very commonly connected with the supposed reduction of the amount of surface water in Lake Eyre and the river and lake systems in its vicinity. It is said that in the good old days when there was a wet season it was always followed by another, showing that the presence of moisture brings about more precipitation.

Now, such statistics as there are, and such enquiries as I have been able to make, do not bear out these stories of deterioration of the country and its rainfall at all. I made extensive investigations in the country from Lake Eyre to Birdsville in 1929 and again in 1939. 1929 was the worst drought year the country had ever known. The- mean recording of the eleven rain gauges then in operation was 1.8 inches, with one station (Mulka) as low as 70 points. Lake Eyre was absolutely dry, just three thousand square miles of pink and dusty slit, and there was scarcely a beast on its feet in the country. The only living things to be found. near the lake were needle bush and crows, and it was hard to find enough needlebush to boil the billy. The waterholes were still holding out on the Diamantina and there were a few cattle remaining on Pandi Pandi.

1939 on the other hand was one of the best seasons ever known in the Dead Heart, with an average of 10 inches of rain over all stations, and the difference in the country was amazing. The Diamantina was running a channel flood, there was some shallow water on parts of Lake Eyre, seabirds were at the lake in flocks, and the whole region was covered with a wonderful growth of herbage and grasses, as has been described above. The Birdsville track had not been in such a condition in the memory of living drovers, and mobs of cattle were pouring down from Queensland. There was fodder in the country for millions of sheep and cattle, but hardly a beast to eat it. The following year, 1940, was again one of the worst on record, with an average rainfall of just over 2 inches at nine recording stations.

The average annual rainfall of the Lake Eyre region is 5 inches, but this figure has little meaning, as the rainfall varies so widely from the average. It is characterized by several drought years in succession when there will be no more than 2 inches in the year, and then perhaps a fall of 12 inches will come. It is better described as 10 inch or nothing country. After the return of the expedition all the rainfall statistics from the Dead Heart available at the Weather Bureau, Adelaide, were examined. Sixteen stations were selected for special study, most of them unofficial gauges on cattle stations, the readings having been made available by the pastoral firms and companies concerned. The stations were Marree, Muloorina, Mulka and Mungeranie along or near the Birdsville track; Kalamurina, Cowarie and Clifton Hills along the Diamantina; Kanowana, Innamincka, and Cordillo Downs in the Cooper Country; Farina and Murnpeowie in the North Flinders Ranges; and Strangways Springs, Coward Springs, Oodnadatta and Charlotte Waters along the railway and telegraph line on the west side of the lake. The records began in 1874 at the telegraph stations at Strangways Springs and Charlotte Waters, and those stations have continued to the present day, if one discounts the move of the Strangways gauge to William Creek in 1896 and the Charlotte gauge to the Finke in 1938, both short moves. Farina records begin in 1879, Muloorina and Cowarie in 1882, Cordillo Downs in 1883, Innamincka in 1884, Marree in 1886, Kanowana in 1890, Oodnadatta in 1892, Murnpeowie in 1893, Clifton Hills in 1894. Cowarie ceased recording in 1901, Muloorina in 1902, and Kalamurina opened in 1884 and closed in 1897. There are gaps in the Clifton Hills records, as the station has been moved or abandoned and then reoccupied, and also in several of the others, notably Kanowana. The records disclose the following facts of special interest. The best general season was in 1920, with an average rainfall over all stations of nearly 12 inches. The next best seasons were 1879, 1885, 1890 and 1939, all with about 10 inches. In 1917 there was an exceptional rain along the Birdsville track with over 13 inches at

Kanowana and Clifton Hills, and over 12 inches at Mungeranie, the only stations recording. In the same year Marree only received 61/2 inches. The maximum readings from all the stations mentioned are 1,599 points at Cordillo Downs in 1890, 1,621 points at Innamincka in 1885, and 1,626 points at Innamincka in 1907. The maximum recording at Marree is 1,145 points in 1939 and at Charlotte Waters 1,231 points in 1908 (100 points is an inch).

The worst general season was 1929 with an average of about 180 points.

Other very bad years were 1900 with 240 points and 1940 with 220 points, but away back in 1876 Charlotte Waters only received 171 points and Strangways Springs 212 points, the only stations recording. The worst year on the Birdsville track was 1888 when only 65 points fell at Cowarie and 70 at Muloorina. Other very bad periods along the Diamantina were from 1898 to 1902 and from 1927 to 1929.

In four cases an exceptionally good season was followed by a second, namely in 1877, 1889, 1909 and 1910. On the other hand, on four occasions, in 1885, 1917, 1920, and 1939, a single good season was followed by a normal poor one, and also in four cases, 1877, 1885, 1889 and 1904 the good season was preceded by an exceptionally dry one.

The only conclusion that can be drawn from the rainfall figures is that the rainfall is extremely erratic. There does not appear to be any rhythm in it. There have been eight good seasons in sixty-two years, which gives an average of about nine years apart, and eight bad seasons in sixty-four years.

There is no evidence that rainfall is deteriorating or that a good season begets a good season. If the latter were true, one good season should initiate an endless series of good seasons, Actually, the recurrence of a good season only means that the conditions of major atmospheric circulation that produced the first have persisted in the next.

Professor J. W. Gregory, the author of The Dead Heart of Australia, visited the country in the summer of 1901-2, a time of drought. The bores had been sunk along the Queensland Road or Birdsville track, but all the cattle stations were closed. Only the Killalpaninna Mission Station was still occupied and that closed soon after. Gregory wrote: "We were now well out on the Queensland Road, and for the first few days of our journey we were lost in admiration of the pluck of the South Australian people in settling here, and at the enterprise of the Government in opening a practicable route across such a desert: it seemed incredible that stock raising could ever have been successful in such a country". Five years later there were two good seasons in succession. Had Gregory seen the country then he would have had a very different and equally erroneous tale to tell. I have had the opportunity of seeing the country both at its very worst and at its very best, and I would say that conditions have not changed since the first white occupation. The history of the country is made up of a series of long droughts broken by short periods of comparatively heavy rain which put the land into good heart for a year or two, from which happy state it slowly but inevitably falls away again till the next rain comes, and these cycles of long droughts and short rains control the occupation or desertion of the holdings. Some stations and managements have lasted out several cycles, some have closed finally after one, some have been reoccupied several times after long breaks.

It is obvious that a rainfall of 5 inches or under is practically useless.

It is only the exceptional rains that bring any profit to the land, so that success must be the exception and not the rule, and that makes it a gamblers' country. It is an exciting game, but can be played with success only by players with the necessary experience, and what is even more important, with sufficient resources behind them to tide them over the lean years.

Stories of the sand drift are exaggerated. There are few obvious signs of this. After coming through the Simpson Desert, where there has been no interference by either rabbits or man, we felt the Diamantina country was very stable, with quite a remarkable absence of live and moving sand. One hears stories of homesteads being drifted over with sand. There may be such, but all I can say is that at all the deserted stations I have seen, namely Kaliduwarry and Annandale on the Mulligan, and Goyder's Lagoon, Mt. Gason, Cowarie, and Kalamurina along the Diamantina, and Muloorina near the Lake, there are no signs whatever of any drift sand piling up round the homesteads. They are no different from the houses in Marree, which is in a completely devastated area. Another persistent story is that the Strzelecki and the Cooper are completely blocked with drift sand and can never run again. We crossed the Cooper near Lake Eyre and its bed was perfectly free. There was no sign of encroaching sandridges, though its course crossed the ridges at right angles. There is also no blocking where the

Birdsville track crosses the Cooper. Jack Bejah had made many trips up the Strzelecki and Cooper, and he declares that there is nothing to prevent the Cooper from flowing again as soon as enough water comes down, and that there is sand in the Strzelecki only at its southern end near Lake Callabonna. The Surveyor-General of.South Aus¬tralia, Mr. C. M. Hambridge, has recently traversed the Strzelecki and confirms Bejah's statement for that river, and Mr. Jack Conrick who has spent most of his life on Napper Merrie Station on the Cooper near Innamincka confirms Bejah for both rivers.

The Cooper reaches Innamincka practically every year, at least as a channel flood, but it must flood literally hundreds of square miles and fill countless branches, channels, billabongs, and lakes, including Lake Hope, before it can reach Lake Eyre. It. is only in times of high flood that water has ever been able to overflow into the Strzelecki. A colossal amount of water must come down before the flood reaches the Birdsville track and Lake Eyre, and such occasions must have peen extremely rare in the last few centuries. The last big flood was in 1918, after record rains and floods in the delta area itself in 1917, when over 13 inches was recorded at several stations. This rain must have at least partially filled the lakes and swamps and left the way open for the Queensland floods. As far as I have been able to ascertain the Cooper also reached the lake or ran in its lower courses in 1891, 1898 and 1906, with 1906 the record flood, but there are no proper records, only the tales of old timers. One such account claims that the water reached Lake Hope eighteen times in the forty-five years preceding 1932. It seems certain that the river will only reach the lake when there are exceptionally heavy rains all along its course, which is half way across the continent.

The Diamantina is quite a different river from the Cooper. It has a single channel all the way to Lake Eyre from Birdsville, except for Goyder's Lagoon, and has no lakes to fill on the way. There is one branch, the Kallakoopah, before the lake is reached, but this is only filled at very high flood. Normally all the water goes down the Warburton, as the main channel is called below the branch. The channel flood reaches Lake Eyre on the average every other year and runs for several months when it is running.

All the evidence indicates that the seasons are no better and no worse than they had been for a very long time before the white man came, and that a good season brings up as much feed as it ever did. Take the example of

Muloorina Station, on the Frome, thirty miles north of Marree and almost on the shores of Lake Eyre. It was opened as a sheep station in 1882 and closed in 1902. The rainfall averaged 407 points in that time with a maximum of 771 points in 1885. The next best was 704 points in 1889. For the last three years of its existence the figures were 204, 267, and 125 points. The Government took it over as a camel depot soon after and abandoned it in about 1929, as the camels were no longer wanted. In 1938 it was reoccupied as a sheep station and enjoyed greater prosperity than it had ever known, and this has continued up to 1944. The rainfall in Marree in 1939 was 1,145 points, its all-time record. Muloorina was certainly not eaten out and destroyed beyond hope of regeneration, though it looked like it when I saw it in 1929. Only rain was required for it to regenerate itself without any assistance or expenditure whatever.

The permanent stock-carrying capacity of the country depends on the perennial shrubs, which are the drought resisters, and they are in very delicate. equilibrium with their environment. They can stand very little interference at all. They are like the aboriginals, in that contact with the white man leads to their extinction. The fattening food is the annuals, and they come up abundantly after every rain. The perennials are soon destroyed and their regeneration is a much slower process, so that, as the permanent stocking depends on them, it seems fair to say that this is practically nil. The actual experience of the country's history bears this out. The region has never been destroyed by overstocking or reduced to a state of drifting sand. The stations closed simply because the droughts were too long to be tided over, The permanent feed was never of any account. At every reopening, and most of the stations have gone through several, things were just as good as ever they were in the early days, when the supposed prosperity was just as short lived. Actually, a lot of the country has still never had any stock on it at all, in areas far from permanent water.

The only way of making any use of this country would seem to be to recognize that prosperity only comes intermittently with the rains, and that it is impossible to carry stock through several successive years of drought. This means that the country must be exploited in good seasons, abandoned in droughts, which was the Kidman way. Whatever may be said of the sheep country, I am convinced that since the white man came, the cattle country of the Cooper and Diamantina has undergone no change in climate and very little in productiveness. Its value was always very low, and far too much was expected of it, a country where the rainfall may be under two inches for several years in succession.

Various schemes have been brought forward for improving this desert region. The oldest is that of letting sea water into Lake Eyre by means by a channel cut from Spencer's Gulf. It was considered by the Government in 1883 and rejected. Gregory in his *Dead Heart* regards it as quite impracticable, and comes to the conclusion that even if the scheme were a success the sheep would need to grow golden fleeces to pay for it. The idea is still brought forward from time to time. It appeals to the imagination but does not bear any close investigation. Actually little is known about the levels of the lakes. The only precise level known is that of the bed of Stuart's Creek at the railway line, thirty-nine feet below sea level. This means that Lake Eyre South is at least that much below sea level along its southern shore. Whether the main area, Lake Eyre North, is higher or lower than the south lake is quite unknown. The surveyor Lewis ran a line of levels out from the shore at the north end of the north lake and found a fall of two and a half feet in seven miles. That is all that is known about levels. However, assuming that both lake beds are forty feet below the sea, one can do some rough calculations on the project of letting the sea in. The distance from Port Augusta to the north lake is 250 miles. The evaporation is 100 inches per year and the net loss of water would be about 85 inches a year, allowing for the slower evaporation of saline water, additions by rainfall, etc. The area is about 3,000 square miles. Thus, to beat the evaporation our canal must carry some 19,000 cubic feet of water per second. With a fall of 39 feet over the distance, a canal a thousand feet wide at the bottom flowing ten feet deep would be required. Lake Torrens would be no help to the scheme, as its bed is 111 feet above sea level, and the country beyond rises up to 200 feet above sea level at the divide between the lakes. The canal would thus be from 100 to 200 feet deep and the cost of its excavation would run into several hundred million pounds. A very important consideration, and one not often foreseen, is that the lake must eventually fill up with salt, as salt would be pouring in all the time. Evaporation is reduced as salinity increases but we may take it as 60 inches over a long period. Sixty inches of sea water contains one inch of solid salt, so that one inch of salt will be deposited annually in the lake. If its depth is ten feet, it will become entirely filled with salt in 120 years. Thus the scheme must pay for itself in a period of something of that order.

The Quatara Depression in the Libyan Desert, recently brought into prominence by the fighting at El Alamein, has been thoroughly investigated from this point of view. The object was chiefly to provide a power supply by the fall of water. There the area is 7,000 square miles, the distance from the Mediterranean only 35 miles, and the fall 200 feet, so that it is an immense potential source of power, with a life dependent on the rate of inflow of water allowed. It was not considered that there would be any appreciable effect on climate and there was not enough demand for power in Egypt to justify the outlay at that time. The fall is too small for Lake Eyre to be used as a source of power in this way.

Meteorologists are unanimous in the opinion that the presence of water in Lake Eyre would not have any noticeable effect on the rainfall. Rainfall depends on the major wind circulations of the globe, and water evaporated in one place may be precipitated half a world away, where conditions for cooling and condensation are suitable. It is practically impossible for the evaporated water to be dropped immediately beside. the evaporating lake or sea, otherwise the Dead Sea, the Red Sea, and many other seas and oceans, would not have such arid and barren shores. It can he argued with more reason that an atmosphere, cooler and moister from the presence of surface waters, will induce more precipitation from passing air masses that have brought their moisture from elsewhere, and there must be some slight effect in this direction, but the question is, how much? In no place in the world can such it beneficial effect be noted. Spencer's Gulf itself does not appear to be of any help to the rainfall in its vicinity. The Flinders Ranges, on the other hand, to the east of the Gulf; have a very marked and obvious effect on the rainfall. The great uncertainty of any appreciable effect whatever on the rainfall, the comparatively short life of the scheme owing to the filling of the lake with salt, and the enormous cost, make it quite impossible to give further serious thought to the project of letting the sea into Lake Eyre.

Almost equally fantastic schemes for the irrigation of the central regions were advanced not long before his death by Dr. Bradfield of Sydney Harbour Bridge fame. One part of these schemes was the construction of four reservoirs at the headwaters of the Finke, Georgina, Diamantina and

Cooper Creek. Each dam was to be 140 miles long, and to impound 5,000 square miles of water 20 feet deep, that is, water which at present can scarcely reach Lake Eyre, was to fill four dams each many. times the holding capacity of Lake Eyre. Another scheme was to bring the waters of the Burdekin River across the Dividing Range by tunnel from the Queensland coast, and discharge them into the Cooper, thus watering western Queensland from Hughenden to the border with a constant stream of 6,000 cubic feet per second. Dr. Bradfield's map shows a circular area of over 600,000 square miles stretching from the Gulf of Carpentaria to Lake Torrens, which could be irrigated by these schemes and would be suitable for growing rice, cotton, flax, jute, maize, wheat, tropical fruits, tea, coffee, sheep and cattle. Dr. Bradfield's figures are astronomical, and his statements fire the imagination, but his schemes are entirely visionary and rest on no firm foundations whatever. His brochure will not bear any close examination. It consists of bald statements not supported by any facts or observations. It is merely good journalism, with no more foundation in fact than the fiction of Ion Idriess. Dr. Bradfield had never visited the places he so liberally irrigates, and he admitted that surveys must be made, and that he had no knowledge of the country of the levels or even the discharges of the rivers. The sand ridges of the Simpson Desert form the core of his irrigated lands. He recommends as a subsidary scheme the damming of the Mulligan River, and taking its waters a hundred miles across to Lake Caroline on the Hay River that traverses the Simpson Desert. Why not use these waters along the Mulligan itself? Transporting waters to another place seems to have been rather an obsession. Dr. Bradfield wrote as though there were no question but that the presence of surface waters increased rainfall, and even went as far as asserting that the whole of the evaporated water would be dropped in the immediate vicinity, so that the same water would be used over and over again!

It is impossible to take Dr. Bradfield's schemes seriously or to regard them as anything but visions having little connection with reality. To fill Lake Eyre from the sea is a useless idea. There is not enough rainfall to revive the river systems, and the impounding of water has limited scope owing to the topography of the country. The diversion of rivers is not to be thought of till after the fullest use has been made of their waters in their own basins. In our post-war reconstruction there are a thousand sound schemes waiting to be carried out at our back doors so to speak, in the way of irrigation, closer settlement, development of brown coal deposits, power schemes, secondary industries, transportation, before we need turn to any hazardous and uncertain plans for the arid interior, which is only poor pastoral country that will never support any considerable population. Its supposed deterioration is really an acknowledgement of its initial poverty. It need not be neglected. More bores should be sunk for water, erosion should be combatted, grazing controlled, pastures improved and soil surveys made; but the Interior should never be looked on as a great asset or as a solution of the population problem, and expenditure on it should be in strict accordance with possible returns, for otherwise we should be forsaking the substance for the shadow. Dreams of increasing the rainfall by impounding water or of making the arid Interior a garden of Eden by irrigation are nothing but castles in the air, with no more substance than Lasseter's Reef, another myth that is kept alive only by the glamour of mystery and inaccessibility that surrounds it.

Journey's end at Marree. Left to right: Hubbard, Nurie, Crocker, District Nurse, Bejah Dervish, Fletcher, Jack Bejah.

www.ingramcontent.com/pod-product-compliance
Lightning Source LLC
Chambersburg PA
CBHW030530020726
47494CB00004B/1295